THE LEGO®
NINJAGO®
MOVIE™

JUNIOR NOVELIZATION

THE LEGO® NINJAGO® MOVIE™

JUNIOR NOVELIZATION

Adapted by **Kate Howard** from the screenplay

Story by **Hilary Winston & Bob Logan & Paul Fisher and Bob Logan & Paul Fisher & William Wheeler & Tom Wheeler**

Screenplay by **Bob Logan & Paul Fisher & William Wheeler & Tom Wheeler and Jared Stern & John Whittington**

Scholastic Inc.

Copyright © 2017 Warner Bros. Entertainment Inc. & The LEGO Group. THE LEGO NINJAGO MOVIE © & ™ Warner Bros. Entertainment Inc. & The LEGO Group. LEGO, the LEGO logo, the Minifigure, the Brick and Knob configurations and NINJAGO are trademarks and/or copyrights of the LEGO Group. Copyright ©2017 The LEGO Group. All rights reserved. (s17)

Published by Scholastic Inc., *Publishers since 1920.* SCHOLASTIC and associated logos are trademarks and/or registered trademarks of Scholastic Inc.

The publisher does not have any control over and does not assume any responsibility for author or third-party websites or their content.

No part of this publication may be reproduced, stored in a retrieval system, or transmitted in any form or by any means, electronic, mechanical, photocopying, recording, or otherwise, without written permission of the publisher. For information regarding permission, write to Scholastic Inc., Attention: Permissions Department, 557 Broadway, New York, NY 10012.

This book is a work of fiction. Names, characters, places, and incidents are either the product of the author's imagination or are used fictitiously, and any resemblance to actual persons, living or dead, business establishments, events, or locales is entirely coincidental.

ISBN 978-1-338-13971-6

10 9 8 7 6 5 4 3 2 1   17 18 19 20 21

Printed in the U.S.A.   40
First printing 2017

Book design by Jessica Meltzer

CONTENTS

It was a bright, cheerful morning in Ninjago City. The citizens of the seaside capital were busy repairing buildings and working together to rebuild their city. They had just suffered yet another attack by the evil warlord, Lord Garmadon.

"*Goooooood morning, Ninjago!*" the people sang happily as they worked. "*I said, good morn-ing, Ninjago! Oh, everybody have a ninja day!*"

Even though rebuilding the city brick by brick was difficult — and thinking about Garmadon was always terrifying — Ninjago's residents were smiling and friendly as they went about their work. "*Oh, everybody have a ninja day!*"

While it was true that a menacing warlord with glowing red eyes and four arms attacked their city a few times each week, the people of Ninjago City had plenty to be happy about. Because they had a Secret Ninja Force that was always ready to keep them safe from danger. Every time Lord Garmadon tried to

conquer the city, the Secret Ninja Force managed to chase him away, along with his army of Sharkmen.

All around Ninjago City, people pitched in with the reconstruction process in whatever way they could. All the while, they sang and shared stories.

We traveled from cities from miles around,
'Cause all our cities burned to the ground.
We came to Ninjago and built this town . . .

The work and singing stopped for a moment as footage of Garmadon's latest attack flashed across a giant Jumbotron in the center of the city. But soon, the people were back at it again — working hard as they reminded one another of the danger that always lurked nearby. They sang:

You should know,
The guy from the volcano is evil Lord
*   Garmadon!*
Conquering on and on . . . GAR-MA-DON!
Knocking our city flat, but we rebuild
*   after that . . .*
Because it's a ninja day!

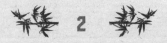

A worried father kneeled in front of his children as they waited for the school bus. "Now, kids," he said quietly. "You know what to do when Lord Garmadon invades, right?"

The kids pumped their fists and shouted, "Duck and cover!"

"That's right! And don't get up until the ninja have given the all clear," their dad reminded them. He waved as the kids hopped aboard the bus. "Have a great day!"

All around the city, people began singing in tribute to Ninjago City's beloved ninja.

Our mystery ninja: They're heroes!
We don't know their names, don't know who
     they are . . .

Inside a coffee shop, the barista passed a steaming cup of tea to a customer. "So, who do you think the ninja are?" she asked in a hushed voice.

Her customer shrugged as he looked up from his phone. "They're, like, some totally sick immortal warriors," he replied.

No one knew exactly who the Secret Ninja Force

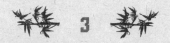

were, but everyone agreed they were awesome. They sang:

We love our citizens, we love every girl
   and boy.
We love all the Secret Ninja
Green, red, white, black, silver, and blue . . .
We like everyone in Ninjago, except for —

Suddenly, a curious face peeked out of a window in an apartment building at the center of the city.

"Good morning, Ninjago!" a teenage boy sang out in a friendly voice.

The songs that had filled the streets only moments before faded, and then stopped completely when people realized who it was looking out over the city: Lloyd Garmadon.

"Sorry, uh . . ." Lloyd waved sheepishly.

Everyone glared up at him.

Lloyd took a deep breath and called out in his most cheerful voice, "Didn't mean to interrupt your song. You were saying, '*We like everyone in Ninjago, except for . . .*'?"

There was a long moment of awkward silence, and then finally someone yelled, "YOU!"

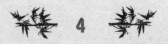

Lloyd sighed, but didn't let his smile slip. He rested his elbows on the windowsill and looked out over the city he loved.

From deep inside the apartment he shared with his mom, Lloyd could hear a TV news report blaring. The reporter said cheerfully, "Annnnd it looks like traffic in Ninjago City has come to an absolute standstill! Everyone in the entire city has stopped to glare up at Lloyd, the kid no one likes. Back to you, Lisa!"

"Okay, well," Lloyd said, his shoulders slumping as he waved feebly to everyone working in the city below him. "Everybody have a ninja day?"

Lloyd shut the window and shuffled into the kitchen to grab some breakfast. As soon as he stepped away from the window, he could hear the muffled sounds of "Good morning, Ninjago!" start up again.

Lloyd sighed. He longed to tell people that he, Lloyd Garmadon — the guy everyone was always mad at! — was actually a member of the Secret Ninja Force. But his identity as the Green Ninja had to remain a secret; otherwise he and the other ninja couldn't exactly call themselves the *Secret* Ninja Force.

"Morning, honey!" Lloyd's mom, Koko, said as

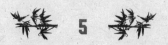

he settled in at the table to eat his breakfast. "You ready for a *great* day?"

Lloyd frowned and cast his eyes to the table. "Not really."

"Aww," Koko said, pinching Lloyd's cheek. "Why's your smile upside down, sweetie? The sun is shining. People are singing!"

Lloyd moped. "People are *always* singing in Ninjago City, Mom. Except around me. They all hate me because I'm Garmadon's son. It kinda brings the vibe down."

Koko chuckled and waved him off. "Oh, that's crazy talk, pumpkin."

Lloyd shook his head. His mom never seemed to notice how much everyone disliked him — even when they were being completely obvious about it!

To prove his point, Lloyd stepped toward the window and heaved it open again. As soon as he did, the singing stopped. Someone yelled up, "Hey, uh, Garmadon Junior? Could you shut that window? You're kinda bringing the vibe down."

He lifted his eyebrows and shot his mom a look, as if to say, "See?"

Koko put an arm around her son. "Okay, fine. So maybe there's a Grumpy Gus or two out there

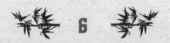

who don't like you because of your dad. But your mom's pretty cool, right?"

"Uh," Lloyd said awkwardly. His mom was nice and sweet and all, but cool? That was a bit of a stretch. "I mean, uh —"

Koko began dancing around the room, singing loudly, "*Moms are great, Moms are cool! Didn't you know that moms are awesome?!*" She grinned at Lloyd and wiggled her hands in the air, and then continued her song.

> *I'll make you pancakes before you go to school,*
> *'Cause I'm your mom and I am cool.*
> *I'm your mom and I am COOL!*

Koko finished her song with a flourish, tossing a heaping platter of breakfast in front of her son — eggs, pancakes, cereal, and toast.

Lloyd dug in gratefully. Even if her songs weren't all that great, his mom's breakfasts were always the best. And they always managed to turn his mood around.

Deep down, Lloyd knew that it was only a matter of time before he would defeat Lord Garmadon

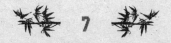

once and for all — and then people would finally realize he was a great guy!

"You know what the coolest thing about moms is?" Koko asked. "They'll always love you. Forever and ever plus forever!" She bent down and planted a huge, sloppy kiss on Lloyd's cheek.

Lloyd stared down into his cereal bowl. The letters in his cereal spelled out:

I LOVE YOU SO MUCH! LOVE, MOM.

Well, at least his mom had his back, even if he was Lord Garmadon's son.

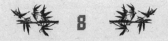

2

After breakfast, Lloyd raced outside to catch the school bus. He stepped slowly up the bus steps, smiling at each of the kids he passed as he made his way down the aisle.

"Good morning," he called, putting on his most chipper voice.

But no one returned his greeting. All around the bus, groups of kids put their heads together and started whispering.

"I can't believe we have to ride all the way to school with him," one girl muttered, casting Lloyd a sidelong glance.

Another rolled her eyes and said, "I know! That kid is the worst. The absolute worst. His dad ruins everything."

A nervous-looking boy slid down in his seat and whined, "He almost looked at me. Did you see that? He came *so* close to looking at me."

9

Lloyd tried to ignore all the whispers and comments. He settled into the first open seat he found. As soon as he'd picked his spot, everyone on that side of the bus leaped up and piled into seats on the *other* side of the bus. The shift in weight caused the bus to tilt to one side as it chugged along toward Ninjago High School.

But Lloyd wasn't deterred. When the bus pulled up at school, he rushed out of the bus and strutted toward the school doors.

"Hey, guys!" he called out, waving to kids he knew from his classes. "Hey, classmates!"

But no one waved back. Everyone just glared at him.

"His dad knocked down my house," one kid said, shooting Lloyd an angry look.

"Yeah," another kid agreed, nodding. "Mine, too."

Luckily, when Lloyd stepped inside the front doors, he immediately spotted one of the few people at school who liked him: Zane, a Nindroid, who was also a member of the Secret Ninja Force.

Zane glanced at his friend, and then scanned both Lloyd and the school hallway using his computer vision.

"Good morning, Lloyd. My sensors indicate

you're suffering from above-average levels of social anxiety," Zane noted.

"No," Lloyd said with a shrug. "It's about average."

Zane nodded. "Prepare yourself, Lloyd. Several spitballs, paper airplanes, and 'Kick Me' signs are incoming."

A moment later, a paper airplane zipped through the sky toward Lloyd's head. The kid who threw it yelled, "Hey, Garma-doofus!"

Just before the tip of the airplane hit him, Lloyd ducked. "Nice throw! Remember, you can't pick your parents, right?" he called.

A few moments later, another kid sneaked up behind Lloyd and tried to stick a "Kick Me" sign onto his back. But before he could press it into place, Kai — another member of the Secret Ninja Force — leaped out of nowhere and pushed the kid out of the way.

"Yo, Lloyd!" Kai said, hugging him. "You need to hug out some negativity?" Kai put his hands on his hips and addressed the kids around them. "Listen up! Anyone who's got a problem with Lloyd, keep walking. Just continue walking. Keep doing exactly what you're doing, which is walking . . ."

A few people grumbled and glared at Lloyd, but no one tried any more mean pranks.

Nya, Kai's sister and another member of the Secret Ninja Force, blasted down the school hall on her supercool motorcycle.

"'Sup, Lloyd?" Nya said, skidding to a stop. She flashed her friend a smile. "Want a lift to class? On my HOG?"

Lloyd cocked his head. "That's okay, Nya. I'd rather —"

But Nya cut him off. She swept Lloyd, Zane, and Kai onto the back of the motorcycle and whooped, "Sweet! Let's ride!"

When Nya screeched to a stop in front of Lloyd's locker, the four friends found the final two members of the Secret Ninja Force — Jay and Cole — waiting for them. As usual, Cole was listening to music on his huge headphones. Jay was leaning on the lockers, waiting for Nya.

"Wow," Jay said, his face filled with awe as he took in Nya's motorcycle. "Nya is so boss."

"Hey, Jay," Lloyd said, holding his hand up for a high five. "Hey, Cole." Lloyd waved to Cole, eager to get his friend's attention. "Can I get to my locker?"

Cole gestured to his headphones. "Sorry, Lloyd. Can't hear you, bro."

"I actually need to get in my locker, Cole," Lloyd said.

"Uh, still nothing, Lloyd," Cole said, ignoring him. "Your lips are moving, but no words are coming out."

"Seriously?" Lloyd said, exasperated.

Reluctantly, Cole removed his headphones and stepped aside. Someone had spray-painted the word "GARMA-DORK" in big letters across the front of Lloyd's locker.

"Okay," Cole said sadly. "I was just trying to look out for you."

Lloyd tried to laugh it off, but it hurt. The hits just kept coming — day after day after day. It was getting harder and harder to have a good attitude.

His friends exchanged a look.

"Don't worry about the spray paint, Lloyd. Jay's scarf can get that right out!" Nya said.

Lloyd knew he was lucky to have his friends who always had his back. "Guys, don't worry about it. I'm okay."

Just then, the cheerleading squad passed the group.

"Ugh, there he is," the head cheerleader said, pointing at Lloyd. "His dad totally ruined my family's

13

Pilates studio two weeks ago. I wonder what his dad's going to ruin this week?"

"What'd you say, ladies?" Nya asked, stepping in front of them. "I can't hear you." She revved the engine on her bike, scaring the cheerleaders away.

"Nice work, Nya," Jay said, smiling fondly at her. His crush on Nya was legendary.

"Anytime!" Nya said, shrugging.

The six friends headed down the hall and into their first class.

"It's all right, guys," Lloyd told his friends as they settled into their seats. "You never know — Garmadon may not even attack today."

Seconds later, an alarm went off.

WAAAAA! OOOOH-WAAAA!

"Oh, no!" their classmates screamed in a panic. "It's Garmadon!"

The kids in class scattered and ran, crying, "Ahh! Garmadon!" and "Lloyd's dad is attacking!" and "Duck and cover, everyone!"

Amid the chaos, Lloyd and his friends shared a look. While most people hurried into hiding, the Garmadon alarm was the ninja's signal to slip into their heroic disguises! It was time for the Secret Ninja Force to get out there and fight.

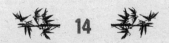

14

Six hands shot into the air at once. Together, Lloyd, Cole, Jay, Kai, Nya, and Zane blurted, "Can I have a bathroom pass?"

Without waiting for their teacher's permission, they raced out of the classroom. As soon as they reached the door, their frightened teacher peered curiously out from under his desk. "Huh. Those kids are always going to the bathroom at the most dangerous times . . ."

Lloyd and the other ninja raced through the hall. Each one stepped into his or her locker. Each locker had a chute that led to the Secret Ninja Force's storage facility inside an enormous warehouse.

As they emerged into the warehouse, Lloyd, Cole, Jay, Kai, Nya, and Zane were disguised in their color-coded ninja outfits. The Secret Ninja Force was ready for battle!

Kai climbed into his Fire Mech and revved the engine. "Red Ninja, fired up!"

Nya, the Silver Ninja, did a few acrobatic flips before she leaped onto the back of her Water Strider.

Cole hopped up into his Quake Mech and geared up his turntables. "Black Ninja. Let's rock!"

Zane scaled the side of his Ice Tank and plugged himself in. "White Ninja: online."

Jay jumped aboard his Lightning Mech and powered it up. "Blue Ninja. Not at all nervous . . ."

Lloyd fired up his Mech Dragon and set the team's coordinates into his dashboard computer. The computer flashed the words:

Target: GARMADON
Weapons: TONS OF SUPERCOOL MISSILES
Objective: MAKE SURE GARMADON NEVER COMES BACK TO NINJAGO CITY!

Lloyd revved his engine and narrowed his eyes. As he and the others zoomed out of the warehouse, Lloyd growled, "Green Ninja, ready for Garmadon. Let's hit it!"

3

As Garmadon's warriors took to the streets of Ninjago City, thousands of citizens fled. Screams pierced the air. All over the city, buildings shook on their foundations, filling the air with dust and smoke. Bricks littered the streets. It was total chaos.

Ninjago City was under attack — again!

A fleet of warplanes buzzed over the city as a giant shark mech emerged from the harbor. Everyone knew that mech far too well. It was Lord Garmadon's personal robot, an enormous attack machine.

"*Good morning, Ninjago...*" Lord Garmadon hummed under his breath. Then he growled, "Ugh, stupid song. It's so catchy — I just hate it!"

Garmadon shook his head to try to get the annoying, upbeat song out of his brain. He guided his mech through the streets, sending bricks flying with each pounding footfall.

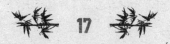

Garmadon laughed maniacally. "What's my name?" he shouted into his megaphone. "It's your favorite warlord! Coming back to conquer! Dominate!"

As Garmadon crashed through the streets, he heard the sweet sound of people screaming his name.

"Garmadon!" A woman gasped.

"It's Garmadon!" a man shrieked.

As Garmadon stormed through the city, he heard his name repeated over and over. The evil warlord took pride in the fact that his was the one name everyone in Ninjago City knew, a name that signified pure evil. Garmadon loved to be feared. In fact, the cries of citizens gasping in awe at his fearsome mech made his heart sing.

"*Good morning, Ninjago!*" he crooned. "*I said, good morning, Ninjago!*" Garmadon growled. He still couldn't shake off that annoying song! "Ugh! Get out of my head!"

He rolled down the window of his mech, getting an earful of the screaming and chaos that surrounded him. "Ah," he said, sighing in contentment. "Much better."

Garmadon looked down and grinned as he

spotted a woman in a white wedding dress scrambling away from him.

"Run!" the woman screamed, grabbing for her new husband's hand. "Run!"

"I'm stuck," her husband said desperately. The man pulled at the leg of his suit, trying to free himself. His leg was wedged between two pieces of fallen debris, and it was clear he was going nowhere.

The groom turned and looked over his shoulder. His face filled with fear when he saw Garmadon's mech stomping closer and closer.

"I love conquering!" Garmadon said, his evil laugh ringing through the streets. "I love conquering this mailbox! I love conquering this fish stand! I love conquering this bride and groom!"

The bride glanced at her husband, and then looked up at Garmadon's imposing shark mech. She dropped her husband's hand. "Honey, I know you want me to save myself . . . so I'll just be going now," she said sweetly. She blew her groom a kiss and then turned and ran as fast as she could. She turned and called back, "I promise I'll never forget you!"

The terrified groom yelled after her, "I didn't ask you to promise that! Come back!" He tugged

at his leg again, but it was no use — he was really, truly stuck. And the shark mech was getting closer by the second.

Other citizens raced past the groom, but no one stopped to help. Everyone was focused on getting to safety before they were blown to bits. It was time to duck and cover!

The groom tugged and pulled at his stuck leg as the air around him filled with smoke. By now, Garmadon was only a few feet away. Through veils of smoke, the man could see the shark mech's penetrating red eyes glaring down at him. He screamed as Garmadon's evil laugh echoed all around.

Just as the evil mech loomed over the groom, ready to stomp him into bits and pieces, the groom felt his body lift into the air. He drew in a breath and looked up. A huge mechanical green dragon was pulling him high into the air, out of Garmadon's warpath!

"Gotcha," Lloyd said, grinning.

Lloyd was pretty sure there was nothing sweeter than saving the day. Quickly but carefully, he guided his Mech Dragon up into the air above the city, pulling the man out of Garmadon's reach. "Congratulations on the nuptials, by the way."

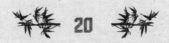

The man whooped. "Thanks, Green Ninja!"

All across Ninjago City, people cheered as the ninja zipped through town. "Ninja!" people whooped. "Whooooooo!"

"Kai and Nya," Lloyd called through his comm link. "You cover the Sushi District. Jay, Zane, Cole: You got Little Manga Town. I'm going after Garmadon."

Lloyd sped away from his friends, blasting at Piranha Mechs and flying manta rays as he weaved through town.

Nearby, Kai was busy blasting Garmadon's army of Sharkmen. "Woo!" he shouted, taking bad guys out one by one. "What's up, bad guys? Come get this FIRE!"

"We love you, Red Ninja!" someone called out from the street below. "You're so hot! Literally and figuratively!"

"Thank you, thank you," Kai said as he torched a swarm of villains. "I love how much you love me!" Through his comm link, he asked his teammates, "Hey, guys, which one of us has the most fans? Definitely me, right?"

Nya rolled her eyes. "It's not a competition, Kai." Unable to resist, Nya scanned the crowd, searching for a few fans of her own. "Look — there's

a Silver Ninja fan! And another one! And several more right there! Ha. So there, Kai!"

Nya pounded her fist on the dash of her vehicle. Then she realized it was time to get back in action. "But just to restate — it's not a competition! I love my job!"

Jay swooped over the crowds below, executing tons of complicated aerial moves in his Lightning Mech. "I'm still not nervous . . ." he said quietly to himself. "I'm operating at maximum confidence level."

Zane rolled toward his teammates. "I have been programmed to kick butt and tabulate names," he announced.

Nearby, Cole spun a record at the DJ table inside his mech. Moments later, he unleashed an ultrasonic sound blast that sent a wave of enemies crashing into a wall. Cole pumped his fist. "REEEE-MIX!" he shouted triumphantly.

As Lloyd raced across the city, eager to catch Garmadon before any more damage was done, his phone began to ring. Lloyd glanced down at the screen. It read: "MOM."

Lloyd cringed, but then he answered. "Uh, hello?"

Koko's terrified voice rang out from the other end

of the line. "Lloyd, your dad — I mean, Garmadon — is back! Are you safe?"

Lloyd held the phone between his ear and his shoulder as he blasted a bad guy heading his way. "Yup. I'm ducked and covered, Mom."

"Great," Koko said, obviously relieved. "And don't worry, Lloyd. The Secret Ninja Force will handle this."

Lloyd tried to come up with an answer, but he drew a blank. He couldn't believe his own mother hadn't figured out his secret identity yet! Before he could reply, Garmadon's evil laugh rang out. "Mwa-ha-ha!"

"Honey?" Koko said. There was panic in her voice. "What was that?"

"Um, nothing," Lloyd lied. "That was nothing. I didn't hear anything at all. It was nothing." In a rush, he added, "Love you, Mom. Bye!" Then he pressed "End Call" and tossed the phone aside.

"All right," Lloyd said, shifting his focus back to fighting his father. He raced toward Garmadon's mech, preparing to blast his evil dad out of town for good.

Just as he reached the evil warlord, he heard his father call out, "Generals, clear a path to Ninjago Tower. Straight ahead!"

Lloyd yelled, "I don't *think* so, Lord Garmadon."

When Garmadon spotted Lloyd's Mech Dragon racing toward him, he called out cheerfully, "Well hello, Green Ninja! Once I plant my flag on that tower, Ninjago City is mine."

"Not gonna happen, Garmadon," Lloyd growled.

"Oh, I'll never stop conquering Ninjago City, Green Ninja," Garmadon shot back. "Because there's something very, *very* special here."

Lloyd took his hand off his missile launch button. "What?" he asked quietly. Was it possible Garmadon was talking about . . . him? "There is?" he asked loudly.

"I'm gonna let the walls down, Green Ninja," Garmadon boomed. "About sixteen years ago, I lost something. Something I should have never given up. Something my life has been incomplete without, and by gosh, I want it back."

"What is it?" Lloyd asked, wide-eyed.

Garmadon held up the fins of his shark mech. "Acres of prime beachfront real estate!" he replied.

"W-w-what?" Lloyd sputtered.

"That's where the warlords make real money," Garmadon explained.

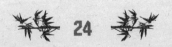

24

"That's it?" Lloyd asked him. "You have no other connection to this city?"

"Look, Green Ninja," Garmadon said, growing impatient. "I have room in my life for exactly one thing: conquering."

"Well, not today, Garmadon!" Lloyd yelled. With the push of a button, Lloyd released the missiles he'd been saving just for his dad.

The weapons hit their target, blasting his dad's mech to pieces — and destroying everything else within a two-block radius.

Garmadon's head poked up out of a smoking crater. He was shaken, but unharmed. Coughing, he told Lloyd, "All right, all right — enough! Good gosh, where did all that come from?"

Lloyd retracted the window of his mech so he could get a better look at his dad. "Just get out of Ninjago City already!" he cried. "And get out of *my life*!"

"Wow," Garmadon muttered, giving Lloyd a funny look. "That's weirdly personal." He paused, and then added, "Fine. I'm going. But I'll be back! And when I return, I'll have something *really* wicked in store for you. Something BIG! Mwa-ha-ha!" He cackled.

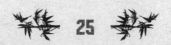

"Oh, I'll be waiting . . ." Lloyd promised. Then he added softly, ". . . Dad."

"I'm sorry," Garmadon said, spinning around. "What was that last thing you said?"

"What?" Lloyd asked.

"That last part," Garmadon said. "I didn't catch it."

"I didn't say anything," Lloyd replied. "What do you mean? I said, 'I'll be waiting,' and then I stopped talking." He paused again, and then whispered, "Dad . . ."

Garmadon shook his head, confused. "Right." Then he faced his army and ordered, "Come! Let's return to my volcanic lair!" Cackling again, he added, "For *now*!"

Garmadon began leading his army out of the city. As he was airlifted to safety, the evil warlord looked back over his shoulder. "Is that kid still looking at me?" he asked one of his generals.

"Yes, sir," his general informed him.

Garmadon cringed. "Ugh, weird. Man, that Green Ninja's got a lot of issues to work out."

After the smoke had cleared, a cop stood in the center of the street and ordered people to head home. The battle was over — for now.

"All right, off you go, everyone. Don't worry if

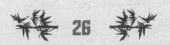

you missed today's excitement. Garmadon will be back again and again and again and again . . ." the cop's voice trailed off.

It was true. The ninja had succeeded in taking Lord Garmadon down once again. But everyone knew the fight wasn't over.

In fact, it had only just begun.

4

After the battle, the Secret Ninja Force returned to the abandoned warehouse where they stored their mechs. Cole, Jay, Kai, Nya, and Zane were eager to celebrate their latest victory over Lord Garmadon.

"Woo!" Cole said proudly. "Guys, today we were so ninja!"

"Yes," Zane agreed. "Quite ninja. Another job well done."

"That was ninjastic," Nya added.

"Coming through!" Kai whooped. "We are all so ninja."

Jay smiled at Nya. "And Nya, the way your smile lights up a room and the sunlight sparkles in your hair is also SO NINJA!"

Cole held up his phone, snapping a series of epic selfies. "This beanie hat is *so ninja*," he bragged, clicking a pic. "And this wallet chain? *So*

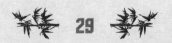

ninja." He posed again. "This half-eaten bagel left over from breakfast? So *ninja*!"

Suddenly, a small rock in the middle of the warehouse floor began to wiggle. Tranquil flute music filled the huge room.

The ninja abruptly stopped their celebration. Nya pointed at the rock and held up a hand. "Guys, guys . . . what is that?"

"I don't remember that rock being there," Cole said, confused.

"Me either," Nya told him.

"That's weird," Lloyd said, stepping a little closer. The rock continued to wobble and wriggle. Then, out of nowhere, Master Wu appeared!

Master Wu was the ninja's wise teacher. He also happened to be Garmadon's brother and Lloyd's uncle.

Wu scowled at his team. "Silence! Students, how many times have I told you, there's nothing *ninja* about you ninja," he said sternly.

"What?" the ninja gasped.

"A ninja master must be invisible," Master Wu pointed out, stroking his long beard. "But you keep blowing everything up with your crazy machines!"

In a flash, Master Wu disappeared.

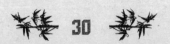

"Whoa!" Cole said, leaping backward. "Where'd he go?"

Just as suddenly, Master Wu reappeared again. "And one with the elements," he added, suddenly transforming himself into a rock. "Like becoming this rock."

"Oooh." The ninja sighed, impressed.

"Ninja are masters of disguise and misdirection," Master Wu declared, popping up behind the ninja.

"Ahh!" Lloyd, Cole, Jay, Kai, Nya, and Zane cried in surprise.

"They must be silent, but deadly," Master Wu continued.

The ninja burst out laughing.

"Why do you always laugh when I say that?" Master Wu asked, puzzled.

"Oh, no reason," said Kai, trying to hide his grin.

"But Master Wu, mechs are so fun," said Nya.

"And awesome," said Kai.

"And convenient," said Zane.

Their teacher shook his head. "Garmadon will be back. Same as last time and the time before that. So you have won nothing."

Lloyd held up a mini-bomb in each hand. "You're

right! That's why I need to re-outfit our mechs with more bombs! Bombs that drop bombs, plus some Swiss Army bombs," he said eagerly. "So that way, the next time Garmadon comes back, we can take him out *forever*."

Master Wu sighed. "Students, weapons are not the answer. True ninja don't rely on mechs and missiles. They practice humility."

"I'm humble," Kai argued. "I'm, like, the humblest guy who's ever been humble!"

"I mean, not as humble as me, but okay . . ." Nya cut him off.

"And bravery," Master Wu added.

"A lot of people would consider this scarf a brave fashion choice," Jay noted.

"And tranquility," Master Wu went on.

Zane held up a hand. "I have been programmed to be tranquil. And literally nothing else."

"And respect," Master Wu said.

Cole pulled off his headphones. "Sorry, what did you say about respect? I wasn't listening."

Master Wu shook his head. He turned to Lloyd. "And most of all, a true ninja must have *balance*. Which you will never have, Lloyd, as long as your heart fills with anger for your father."

Lloyd gritted his teeth. "You mean, the evil,

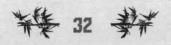

city-destroying warlord who ruins my life on a daily basis? *That* father?"

"Yes." Master Wu nodded. "Him."

"But, Master Wu," Nya argued. "We just *beat* Garmadon. Didn't you see?"

Kai grinned. "It was SO NIN —"

Master Wu cut him off. "Please. I know what you're about to say and just . . . don't. As a ninja master, I've got all kinds of weapons . . ."

Their teacher began to pull dozens of assorted weapons out from behind his back, under his beard, inside the shirt of his gi.

The ninja all gaped at him, astonished at the sheer number of things their teacher had been hiding from them.

"Big weapons," Master Wu said, "little weapons, sharp weapons, dull weapons. I've even got the Ultimate Weapon. But what matters is that you are *balanced*."

"Whoa, whoa, whoa!" Lloyd yelped. "What did you just say?"

"What matters," Master Wu repeated, "is that you are balanced."

"No, no, no," Lloyd said. "The thing before that."

"You mean . . . *the Ultimate Weapon*?" Master Wu said.

The ninja all stared at him, their mouths hanging wide open.

"Um," Lloyd said, the first to speak. "You've been hiding that information *why*?"

"Because the Ultimate Weapon is too dangerous," Wu told them. "That is why I keep it in the most secure, heavily protected place possible . . ." He lifted his straw hat the tiniest crack, giving his team a brief glimpse at the Ultimate Weapon. ". . . under my hat. In the wrong hands, it could spell doom for Ninjago."

"Then put it in my hands," Lloyd cried. "Why does it matter *how* we beat Garmadon, as long as we beat him?"

Master Wu shook his head sadly. "Nephew, until you learn to have balance in your life, *your* hands are the *wrong* hands."

Lloyd glared at Master Wu. He was angry, hurt, and frustrated.

"Lloyd, come with me," Master Wu said, taking his arm.

"Oooh," the other ninja said, snickering. It looked like Lloyd was about to get a lecture from their teacher. And one-on-one to boot.

Master Wu spun around and snapped, "Ninja! Strike balance pose."

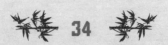

Cole, Jay, Kai, Nya, and Zane grunted, struggling to strike individual balance poses. As he stepped out of the room, Master Wu called back to them, "For seven hundred minutes!"

There was a collective groan from the ninja.

Master Wu ignored them and led Lloyd to the deck of the *Destiny's Bounty*, the intricate and ancient ship that served as the Secret Ninja Force's headquarters.

Lloyd looked at his uncle, and then hung his head. "Master Wu, you don't understand."

"I understand, Lloyd," Master Wu said gently, placing his hand on Lloyd's shoulder. "Garmadon is my brother. I, too, feel responsible for the safety of Ninjago City. But, nephew, I will not always be here. Because I am super old. So you must listen to me when I say . . ." He took a deep breath. "You are winning the battle on the outside, but you are losing the battle on the inside. Destruction is not the ninja way. To achieve balance, you must learn to think differently."

Sometimes, Lloyd thought, his uncle just didn't get it. This was *Lord Garmadon* they were talking about — Lloyd's dad, the source of all his shame and embarrassment and sadness. The only way to beat a bad guy was to *fight* him, and Lloyd was

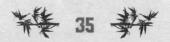

determined to take the evil warlord down once and for all. Because Garmadon was his dad, Lloyd felt it was his personal duty to get rid of him.

Finally, Lloyd said, "Uncle Wu, I don't care if I have balance in my life. I just want to be normal."

"You have had a lot of hard knocks in life," Master Wu acknowledged. "Some of them pretty hard. Why don't I play you a song? Perhaps it will speak to you."

Lloyd had no interest in listening to one of his Master's calming flute songs, but he stayed and listened politely for a few minutes. Then he found the first excuse he could to leave the *Destiny's Bounty* and make his way toward home.

5

As Lloyd weaved through the streets of Ninjago City, he watched people work together to rebuild the city again. The sounds of citizens crooning *"Good evening, Ninjago City . . . everybody have a ninja day,"* filled his ears.

But every time Lloyd passed a group of people, the singing stopped and everyone glared at him. They stared and whispered, just like everyone always did.

Lloyd sighed. He was sick and tired of being the guy everyone hated.

When he stepped into his apartment, Lloyd could hear a newscaster on the TV reporting, "And thank gosh for the Secret Ninja Force, who once again saved our city with a combination of super-cool missiles and well-timed explosions!"

That made Lloyd smile. He wandered into the living room, where he found his mom watching TV.

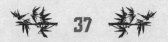

"But I have a feeling," the newscaster went on as Lloyd took off his shoes and put his things away, "that Ninjago City hasn't seen the last of Lord Garmadon, aka the father of Lloyd Garmadon, that kid no one likes."

Lloyd winced. The hits just kept coming.

"Hi, honey," Koko said.

"Hey, Mom," Lloyd said.

"Aw, sweetie," Koko said, standing up to give him a hug. "Turn that frown upside down. I made your favorite." She dashed into the kitchen, singing,

Dinner pancakes when you're home from
    school!
'Cause moms are great and moms are cool!
Moms are great and moms are COOL!

"Ta-da!" Koko slid a heaping plate of food in front of Lloyd and shrugged. "It's a little more than pancakes."

Lloyd looked down at his plate. The food looked delicious, but he just wasn't feeling it. "I'm not really hungry, Mom," he said apologetically.

"Cheer up, sweetie," Koko said kindly. "Better days are ahead."

Lloyd plunked onto the couch. "Mom, can we talk about something?"

"Sure, pumpkin pie," Koko said. "About what?"

"Garmadon."

Koko hesitated. "Okay . . ."

"When you guys got together," Lloyd began, "was Dad, like, a regular guy? Or was he always an evil warlord, or . . . ?"

Koko waved him off. "Lloyd, we've been over this."

"Yeah, but what did you see in him?" Lloyd pressed. "Were you guys in love? How do you love a warlord?" He took a deep breath and pleaded, "I just . . . I need to know."

Koko looked at her son seriously. Then she nodded. "Well, it's really a pretty boring story. We met at work. I was a defensive strategist and he was in hostile takeovers."

Koko smiled as she thought back to her early romance with Garmadon — their romance had been so thrilling!

"He was fearless, aggressive, and really, really tall," she went on. "To be honest, I was kind of into bad boys back then. And no matter what, he could always make me laugh." Koko grinned, and then cackled, "Mwa-ha-ha-ha!"

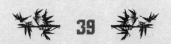

Lloyd shuddered. As far as he was concerned, that laugh sounded the *opposite* of romantic, but he was willing to go with it. He and his mom hardly ever talked about his dad. And even weird information was better than *no* information.

"He was so ambitious," Koko continued. "He said I was his partner in crime and we were going to conquer the world together. I just didn't know he meant it *literally.*" Koko stared wistfully into space. "So unfortunately, your dad is an evil warlord. But something great came out of our relationship: you. You just have to spin your perspective." She put her arm on Lloyd's shoulder. "Right?"

Lloyd considered this for a moment. "Thanks, Mom."

He headed to his bedroom, thinking. His mom had answered *one* question, but there was still a lot more Lloyd longed to learn about the father he had never known. And he had every intention of finding out every last thing about Garmadon that he possibly could.

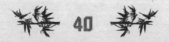

6

Garmadon's secret lair was tucked deep inside a volcano on a rugged, dangerous island. Inside the war room at the heart of his evil headquarters, the warlord casually sipped a cup of tea.

As he waited to start his morning briefing, Garmadon struck up a conversation with a few of his shark-headed generals. "Well, generals. How's everyone feeling this morning?"

Garmadon's team of generals looked around the room, trying to figure out how they should respond. Garmadon wasn't usually a smile-and-chat kind of guy . . . what was going on?

"I'm feeling . . ." began General Number One. "Uh, pretty good?"

"Oh, really?" Garmadon said sweetly. "'Cause you want to know something?"

"Sure!" said General Number One.

"I feel terrible," snapped Garmadon.

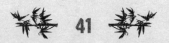

"Oh," the general said, shrinking in his seat.

"Yet again we were defeated by the Secret Ninja Force. And I was up all night trying to figure out why. And I suspect it's because the troops are poorly motivated. So I was thinking . . . what if we just fired a hundred of the men?" Garmadon said.

"Fire them, sir?" asked General Number One.

"Out of the volcano," Garmadon said. "Fire them out of the volcano."

The group of generals looked at one another in alarm.

"Yeah, it just . . ." Garmadon continued, waving all four of his hands in the air, ". . . might help to inspire the others. You know, just give 'em purpose."

General Number One paused. "That's a, uh, fantastic idea, sir. Um, but, wouldn't that be a catastrophic loss of men? You know what I mean?"

"Of course," Garmadon said. "Yes. Good note, General Number One. So maybe we could just fire, maybe, *one* guy out of the volcano?"

"I don't hate it!" agreed General Number One.

"Great," Garmadon said, decided. "Guards!"

Two huge guards stepped out of the shadows.

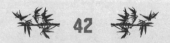

Garmadon pointed to General Number One and ordered, "Fire him out of the volcano!"

The guards dragged the screaming General Number One away.

"Please, sir!" the general pleaded. This was *not* what he had been suggesting! "I have a family. I'm begging you. I have a family!"

Garmadon ignored the former general's protests. He turned to another general sitting at the table. "You! What's your title?"

"Me?" asked the general, who was wearing an eye patch. "I'm General Number Two, sir!"

"Well, now you're General Number One," Garmadon announced.

The eye-patch general looked surprised. "Oh . . ."

Garmadon pointed to another general. "And you, what's your title?"

"General Number Three."

"Well, now you're General Number Two," Garmadon said. "You see where I'm going with this? I told the Green Ninja I was coming back with something big, something *wicked*. Something with some . . . *pizazz*. So, any ideas?"

Garmadon looked out at his team of generals, waiting for a spark of genius.

Instead, he got total silence.

"Come on, people!" Garmadon urged. "This is a safe place. I'm not going to *kill* anyone for a bad idea . . ."

Just then, one of Garmadon's IT experts stepped forward. He had been waiting for the right moment to tell Lord Garmadon about a new mech he and his team had been working on. It shot live sharks out of tanks built into its arms, and it was bigger and more powerful than anything they had built for Lord Garmadon before. This felt like just the time to debut it! "Excuse me, Lord —"

Garmadon slammed one of his fists on the table. "Nerd! You're interrupting!"

"S-s-sorry, sir," stammered the expert. "But we just cooked this up in engineering."

He handed Lord Garmadon a tablet bearing an image of their new creation. This powerful shark mech made Garmadon's previous mech look like a toy meant for toddlers.

"Give me that," Garmadon said, pulling the tablet out of his expert's hands. He eyed the image and grinned. "Oooh . . . Garma-daddy likey!"

"We call it the Garma Mecha Man," the IT expert told him.

At the back of the war room, a bunch of experts

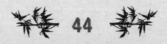

and engineers gave one another high fives. The boss liked it! The engineers had been working so hard on this invention, and getting Garmadon's approval was never a guarantee. (In fact, it almost never happened.)

"Fabulous name," Garmadon said. "Trademark it immediately." He slammed the tablet down on the table and stood up. "Everyone! Prepare for battle!" he barked.

"Yes, sir!" the generals replied.

"Steep more tea!" Garmadon ordered.

"Steeping!" shouted General Number Two, running off to put on the kettle.

"And fire that general!" Garmadon yelled.

A moment later, Garmadon's former General Number One was tossed into the giant volcano. On the evil warlord's cue, the volcano erupted, and the former general went flying deep into the wilds of the jungle.

Lord Garmadon grinned. He loved motivating his troops by making examples of them. *So long, General*, he thought gleefully.

Garmadon hoped this would show his team that he would stop at *nothing* to prove his power.

"Now . . ." he said, drumming all twenty of his fingers together. "Let's go get our conquer on!"

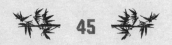

7

Back in Ninjago City, the ninja had returned to the daily grind of their regular lives. With Garmadon out of the picture — for now — it was time to get back to being ordinary teenagers.

"Good morning, class!" said Mr. Peterson, joyfully greeting all the kids in his history class. "Our lesson today is on history's worst tyrants. So put away your books, kids, because we'll be watching a video. It's about the wicked deeds of Lord Garmadon, whose name is synonymous with *eeeeeevil.*"

Dramatic music echoed throughout the classroom as Garmadon's cackling face filled the screen.

While the video showed Lord Garmadon's most evil moments, the narrator's voice rang out, "What makes a man into a monster? Consider Lord Garmadon, whose invasions are a part of everyday life in Ninjago City. Nothing can satisfy Garmadon's

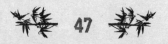 47

insatiable lust for power. And nothing can stop his relentless attacks. He'll keep coming back again and again and again. The good people of Ninjago City will just have to keep rebuilding day after day, brick after brick, over and over and over . . ."

Lloyd let himself zone out as the movie droned on and on. Soon, his mind began to wander. What would it be like, he wondered, to be the ultimate hero? He thought about how awesome it would feel to pull off his Green Ninja mask and let everyone see that it was him — Lloyd Garmadon! — who had helped save the city from Lord Garmadon all those times.

If only I could get my hands on the Ultimate Weapon, Lloyd thought. *I could use it to defeat Garmadon once and for all . . . and save Ninjago City forever!*

That's when Lloyd began to formulate a plan . . .

Suddenly, an alarm sounded, interrupting his reverie. All around the classroom, kids were throwing balls of crumpled-up paper at him.

"Garmadon is attacking us again. You know what to do, kids: duck and cover!" Mr. Peterson instructed the class.

Lloyd, Cole, Jay, Kai, Nya, and Zane exchanged

significant looks. In unison, they called out, "Can I have a bathroom pass?"

Out in the hallway, the six teenagers raced down the hall. Once they'd reached their lockers, they put their hands together and cried, "*NINJA-GO!*"

The Secret Ninja Force leaped into their lockers and were transported to the warehouse. Moments later, they were ready for action.

"Red Ninja, fired up!" cried Kai.

"Black Ninja," Cole yelled, "amped up!"

"Silver Ninja," Nya shouted, "hear me roar!"

"White Ninja," Zane announced, "online."

Jay gulped. "Blue Ninja, still not nervous . . ."

There was a pause while the ninja waited for Lloyd's battle cry. But the Green Ninja was silent.

After a moment or two, the others glanced over. That's when they realized Lloyd was missing.

"Where is Lloyd?!" Nya growled.

No one had any idea where the Green Ninja was. But they couldn't lose any more time waiting for him. They had to get moving.

"He'll have to catch up," Kai said. "Come on!"

As they approached the city skyline, Nya called over her comm link, "Garmadon's headed for Ninjago Tower. Where is Lloyd?"

"I don't know," Jay said, his voice shaking. "But I'm starting to get pretty scared."

All the ninja would have been pretty scared if they realized where Lloyd was. None of them had the faintest idea that Lloyd had devised his *own* plan for defeating Garmadon once and for all — and it involved a little something called the Ultimate Weapon.

ut on Ninjago Beach, hundreds of vacationers were busy enjoying a beautiful afternoon frolicking in the sun and waves. At first, they didn't notice that trouble was brewing in the ocean.

As he prepared for his grand entrance, Garmadon was nearly bursting with excitement. He couldn't wait to debut his new mech. He was eager to show the ninja — especially that *Green* Ninja — his newest creation!

Garmadon waited until the perfect moment, and then he rose slowly out of the water in his new and improved Garma Mecha Man. The evil warlord strode onto the beach and lumbered across the sand. As he did, he opened the mouth of the suit, and water poured out of the shark's jaws.

Beachgoers screamed when they saw who was riding high inside the suit. "Garmadon!" they all yelped. "Run!"

Garmadon sputtered and coughed — he'd had to hold his breath under the water. His new mech was awesome, but it clearly had a few flaws. Through his comm link, he said, "Nerds! Come in, nerds!"

"Yes, Lord Garmadon?" the chief engineer replied.

"There's a slight design flaw in this Garma Mecha Man. I'm soppin' wet!"

"I'll give the note to the team, sir," the engineer promised.

Garmadon stopped and surveyed the crowds on shore. Grinning wickedly, he took a sip out of the soda cup that he'd propped up in the mech's dashboard cup holder. He hit a button inside his suit and blasted dozens of live sharks out of the mech's left arm. "Best. Conquering. Ever!" he announced triumphantly.

Garmadon marched across the sand and then strode toward the city. An army of sea creature-themed mechs trailed after him.

Ninjago City's citizens screamed and ran for cover. But there was no use hiding — Garmadon was ready to take down this town. For *good* this time.

"This is amazing!" Garmadon said when he finally reached the foot of Ninjago Tower in the city

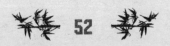

center. "I've never made it this far before! I feel so alive!"

He stopped for a break, huffing and puffing. He was exhausted from the effort of driving his mech through the city. Though the Garma Mecha Man was cool and high-tech in many ways, Garmadon had to pedal the machine like an exercise bike to get it to move.

"Nerds!" he barked into his comm link. "Second design flaw — my quads are killing me!" He set down his staff and did a few leg stretches.

Once he'd caught his breath, Garmadon continued toward the tower. "Woo! Okay, all right. I'm preparing to ascend Ninjago Tower and officially conquer the city. Keep those ninja busy until I can get a shot at them."

The new General Number One replied, "Copy that!"

Garmadon tugged at a few levers, enabling his mech's feet to cling on to the outside of the tower. In the Garma Mecha Man, Garmadon could literally walk up walls!

But just as he began to ascend the tower, his soda slipped out of its cup holder and splashed Garmadon in the face. "Ugh! Nerds! *Another* design flaw."

He wiped the sticky soda away off his face and climbed on. As soon as he reached the top of the tower, Garmadon pumped the mech's arms in the air, shouting, "Wait till the Green Ninja sees my new weapon. This beats *anything* in his arsenal." He laughed maniacally.

Across the city, Cole called into his comm link, "Garmadon is walking up the tower!"

"He's on the fifteenth floor," Kai said in a panic.

"Now he's on the twenty-seventh floor!" Jay yelped.

"Garmadon has just reached the forty-third floor," Zane said calmly.

"He's gonna make it to the roof!" Nya gasped. "Lloyd, come in. We need you!"

"My gosh!" Garmadon said, breathing heavily as he stepped onto the tower's roof. "I've done it! I'm finally atop Ninjago Tower!" He blasted a few sharks into the air to celebrate. "This is it, Ninjago City! I am officially the greatest warlord of all time." He pulled out one of his conquering flags and began to plant it into the roof of the tower.

Suddenly, the Green Ninja's voice rang out from behind the evil warlord. "Stand down, Garmadon!"

Garmadon spun around to face the Green Ninja

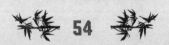

and sneered. Then he noticed the annoying ninja was holding something in his arms.

Garmadon faltered for a moment. "Green Ninja?! Is that . . . the legendary *Ultimate Weapon*?" Garmadon glanced from Lloyd to the Ultimate Weapon and then back again. "But I was going to . . . and then you . . . so now I . . . ugh," whined Garmadon. "This is not fair."

Lloyd hopped off his Mech Dragon and hoisted the Ultimate Weapon onto his shoulder. "Garmadon," he said, pointing the weapon at his adversary. "I'm sick and tired of you trying to conquer Ninjago City. I hereby command you to leave this city. Forever."

Garmadon nodded. "All right, all right." He pretended to consider the Green Ninja's command. "You win. Listen, calm down. You don't have to use that thing."

Lloyd studied him. "So you're going to leave Ninjago City . . . forever?"

"Sure, sure, sure," Garmadon said, holding his hands up in surrender. "Whatever you want. Just be cool, man. Okay? Look, I'm handing over my flags . . ." He began pulling flags out of the Garma Mecha Man. He threw them onto the ground. "Let's

just keep this interaction very chill, okay? I'm chill, you're chill. We're both super chill."

Lloyd's finger hovered over the firing mechanism. "It's over, Garmadon. And now everyone in the city will know that the person who finally defeated you . . . was me." Lloyd ripped off his ninja mask, revealing his true identity. ". . . *Dad.*"

Garmadon's eyes went wide with shock. The Green Ninja was . . . "La-loyd?!"

"That's right," Lloyd told him. "Your son. And it's *Lloyd*!"

"No," Garmadon said seriously. "It's *La*-loyd. L-L-O-Y-D. I named you."

"You ruined my life!" Lloyd screamed.

"Pfft," Garmadon said, rolling his eyes. "That's not true. I haven't even been a part of your life. How could I ruin it? I wasn't even there."

Lloyd glared at him, his hands tightening around the Ultimate Weapon. "Just get out of Ninjago City forever or I'll —"

Garmadon cut him off. "Lemme stop you right there, La-loyd. I must admit, when I saw the Green Ninja holding the Ultimate Weapon, I was a little concerned. But now that I know it's just you . . ."

Lloyd's expression hardened. "I'm serious," he

hissed. "I command you to leave this city or . . . I'm gonna use this."

Garmadon chuckled. "Pfft. Please. We both know you're not gonna shoot your old man."

"Yes, I will," Lloyd promised.

"I just don't see it happening," Garmadon scoffed. "I really don't. I mean, I get what you're going for here — I just don't buy it."

"This is your last chance!" Lloyd warned. "Get out of Ninjago City now!"

Suddenly, dozens of helicopters were hovering overhead. Lloyd kept one eye on Garmadon and the other trained on the fleet of generals landing on the rooftop behind their boss. They were all armed. As a unified pack, they closed in around Garmadon and Lloyd.

Lloyd was dreadfully outnumbered — and since he hadn't told the rest of the team where he was going, he couldn't even call on the other ninja for help.

"Look, La-loyd — this has been cute and all, but I don't have time for it. Put down the Ultimate Weapon," Garmadon ordered. He raised his conquering flag and prepared to plant it into the rooftop again. "I've got a city to CONQUER! And

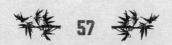

now, introducing your supreme warlord leader, Garma —"

Lloyd gritted his teeth. Then, without another moment's consideration, he fired Master Wu's Ultimate Weapon.

Everyone gasped as a bright-red laser beam shot out and hit Garmadon squarely in the chest.

Garmadon blinked in surprise. But nothing happened.

"You fired it," Garmadon said, impressed. He stepped to the side as Lloyd fired again.

Garmadon ducked out of the way, and the Ultimate Weapon's laser beam hit a skyscraper across the city. The bright-red point of light glowed on the building's surface.

Lloyd pressed the button again and again and again — he was desperate to destroy Garmadon for good. But the red light didn't seem to do anything.

Lloyd shook the Ultimate Weapon. Nothing.

He pushed the weapon's button again. Still nothing.

It was just a glowing red laser — that didn't *do* anything.

"It's not a laser cannon," Garmadon said, sneering as he realized what was going on. "It's a beacon."

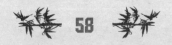

Welcome to Ninjago City, a peace-loving town that is nearly always under attack from the evil Lord Garmadon.

Fortunately, the city is under the protection of the Secret Ninja Force — a group of six fierce high school students.

COLE   KAI

LLOYD

NYA

JAY

ZANE

Recently, Garmadon sent his Shark Army to attack Ninjago City again.

The Secret Ninja Force used their cool mechs to protect the city's citizens.

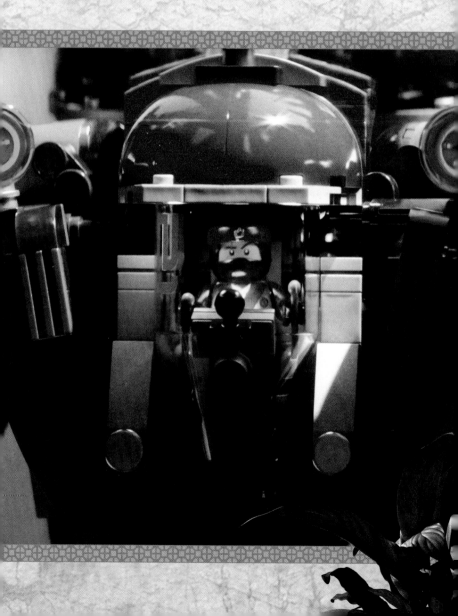

But Garmadon promised he'd return.

Lloyd and the other ninja knew Garmadon would never quit. They vowed they'd be ready for his next attack!

The ninja returned to their secret base to train with their teacher, Master Wu.

Will the Secret Ninja Force find the strength to defeat Lord Garmadon once and for all?

Both Lloyd and Garmadon went silent as a great booming sound echoed through the city.

Thum!

Thum!

Thum!

All around the city, people stopped fleeing and stared up at the sky, trying to find the source of the sound.

Suddenly, an enormous creature began crashing through the streets. The creature lashed out at the red laser point on the side of the skyscraper. The building crumbled like it was nothing more than a sand castle under a child's foot.

There was a moment of stunned silence. Then people screamed and began running again, only faster this time.

"You've awakened the unstoppable beast!" Garmadon said, cackling. "You have summoned . . . the Six-Toed Beast from regions beyond!"

Garmadon hopped out of the Garma Mecha Man suit and raced toward Lloyd. "Let go of it, La-loyd," he said, grabbing for the Ultimate Weapon. "Give me the weapon before it's too late!"

"No!" Lloyd snapped. He knew he couldn't let the Ultimate Weapon fall into his father's hands.

But Garmadon was determined. "Generals!

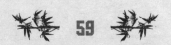

Grab that beacon!" Garmadon knew that if *he* could control the Ultimate Weapon, he would be finally, truly unstoppable!

As Lloyd and Garmadon's henchmen wrestled for control of the weapon, the beam of red laser light flickered from building to building across Ninjago City. The massive beast chased after the light as it moved, knocking over building after building. The entire city was crumbling!

Suddenly, Lloyd lost his grip on the Ultimate Weapon and it slipped out of his hand. It sailed off the edge of Ninjago Tower and landed on a ledge below, just out of reach.

The laser beam's light landed on a disco ball inside a nightclub. Red flashing lights illuminated the city.

The Six-Toed Beast went crazy, jumping from red beam to red beam. It was intent on destroying everything in its path ... including the other ninja, who were all racing to help Lloyd atop the tower.

"No!" Lloyd screamed, realizing too late that his friends were in serious trouble.

"What the heck?" Cole yelped as the beast pounced on top of his Quake Mech. Cole's vehicle

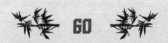

flew sideways before crashing down onto the pavement below.

Seconds later, the Six-Toed Beast had turned toward Kai.

"Nobody help me!" Kai hollered into his comm link. "I got this! I'm good — oof!" The creature pounced on Kai, taking him and his Fire Mech down.

Next, the creature swatted Jay's Lightning Mech out of the sky. Jay ejected from his seat just in time to yell, "*So* not cool, Lloyd!"

Nearby, Nya braced herself as the cockpit of her Water Strider shook violently. The beast lifted Nya's mech up and began ripping it to pieces.

"What is this thing?!" Nya gasped. She, too, pressed the "Eject" button and escaped to safety.

Zane watched helplessly as the giant creature turned toward him. It trampled Zane's Ice Tank, and then headed straight for the Ultimate Weapon.

With one angry swipe, the Six-Toed Beast destroyed the weapon.

But the damage was already done. Ninjago City was in shambles.

Garmadon turned and gave Lloyd a satisfied smirk. "Look at what you've done, La-loyd. You

really are unhinged. Ninjago City lies in ruins. Because of you. That was some pure warlord madness."

Lloyd hung his head in shame. This hadn't gone according to his plan. Not even close.

"Get a load of this kid," Garmadon told his generals. He gazed at Lloyd proudly. "Takes after his old man."

"But I —" Lloyd began. He yanked his arms free from Garmadon's generals and raced to the edge of the building.

When he looked out over the crumbling cityscape, it felt like his heart would break. Sure, Garmadon had damaged Ninjago City time and again. But never had the evil warlord wreaked destruction like this.

The city lay in smoldering ruins. And it was all Lloyd's fault.

Lloyd had made a mistake. He never should have stolen the Ultimate Weapon from Master Wu! And he never should have fired it — what had he been *thinking*?!

He shook his head and took a deep breath. Then he stepped right up to the edge of the building. He knew what he had to do. He had to fix this

situation. But first, he had to get away from his father — fast.

Lloyd stepped toward the edge of the tower. Then he turned back to face Garmadon. "*I wish you weren't my father!*" he cried.

9

Lloyd scrambled as he fell toward the ground, wrapping his hands around a colorful banner hanging off the edge of the building. He managed to snag a corner of the fabric, which turned it into a parachute that delivered him safely to the ground.

Lloyd had a few long moments to think about all the problems he had caused as he drifted toward the ground. Master Wu would be very disappointed in him, and he could only imagine what the other ninja would say about him deploying the Ultimate Weapon.

But this was no time to mope and brood. The other ninja were still in danger, and Lloyd knew he had to help. It was the only thing he could do to make amends for his mistake.

Lloyd came to a gentle landing on the street below Ninjago Tower. He began sprinting through the streets, looking for his friends.

He spotted Nya's broken Water Strider atop a building. But when he looked inside, he saw that the Silver Ninja was gone.

"Nya . . ." Lloyd said, searching for any sign of his teammate.

Cole's Quake Mech hung lifelessly from another rooftop. The Black Ninja's headphones dangled from a piece of scrap metal.

"Cole . . ." Lloyd sobbed.

Lloyd rounded another corner and spotted Kai's Fire Mech sprawled in the street, stray bricks scattered around it.

"Kai . . ." Lloyd whispered through tears.

They were all gone. Had the Six-Toed Beast destroyed his friends? Lloyd raced toward the *Destiny's Bounty*, hoping Master Wu would be able to help him.

When he finally picked his way through the rubble-strewn streets, he found all the other ninja gathered on the ship's deck. They were shaken, but very much alive.

"Oh my gosh!" Lloyd said, relieved. "You guys are okay! That's amazing! That's incredible! That's so . . ."

Lloyd waited for the others to chime in and say "NINJA!" But no one said anything. They just stared at him sternly.

"So *what*, Lloyd?" Nya asked, glaring at him.

"Yeah," Kai said, nodding. "Complete that thought."

"C'mon," Cole said. "I'm listening."

Lloyd said nothing. He just hung his head, and then whispered, "So . . . ninja?"

"Nope," Nya snapped. "This is not *so ninja*. Because instead of fighting Garmadon with us, you used the Ultimate Weapon!"

Jay sighed. "And now Ninjago City is in ruins!"

Zane shook his head. "I have no idea what betrayal feels like, but I imagine it must be something quite close to this."

"That was so NOT ninja," Cole grumbled. "So NOT ninja, Lloyd. Emphasis on the *not*!"

Suddenly, a reed floated through the air in front of the ninja.

"Hey, I don't remember that reed being there . . ." Nya murmured.

A moment later, Master Wu emerged from the water. He held up a hand, silencing everyone. "I'm so disappointed in you, Lloyd. Because of you, the Six-Toed Beast has taken our city. She will show no mercy. She cannot be reasoned with. And her reign of terror will stretch on and on . . . until all of Ninjago City is destroyed.

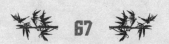

"There is only one hope. One thing that can drive the creature away."

There was a dramatic pause.

"What is it?" Jay asked.

"The Ultimate *Ultimate* Weapon," Master Wu said gravely.

"An Ultimate *Ultimate* Weapon?" Lloyd said. "That sounds even more awesome than the Ultimate Weapon!"

"It is," Master Wu agreed. "That's why it resides in the most secure, most impossible-to-penetrate place in the world . . ."

"Under your hat again?" Jay guessed. "Look how well that worked out."

"No," Master Wu said. He pointed to the horizon. "Hidden where only a true ninja master can find it. On the other side of the island. Through the deadly Forest of Whispers. Past the monstrous Cyclops of Despair. Across the gruesome Valley of Madness. And atop the Temple of Fragile Foundations."

The ninja squirmed with anxiety.

"That does sound difficult," Kai noted.

"And terrifying!" Jay said.

Lloyd stepped forward. "The journey sounds

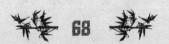

difficult," he said, facing his friends. "But you know what? We're ready."

"No," Master Wu said, shaking his head. "You are not. Your mechs and machines are powerless to help you now. This journey will require the skill of a true ninja. And there's nothing ninja about you ninja. So . . . bye!" He turned and began walking away.

Lloyd hurried after him. "Wait, Master. Please. Take us with you. I know I let Ninjago down."

"It's true," Jay said. "Lloyd let Ninjago down." He cocked his head at Lloyd and whispered, "Sorry, dude." He turned to Master Wu and added, "But we want to fix his terrible mistake."

"Train us to be true ninja," Kai begged.

"Teach us how to be invisible," Nya added.

"And become one with the elements," Jay said.

"And be silent but deadly," Zane put in.

Cole giggled. "I'm sorry," he said. "That's just never not going to be funny."

Lloyd stood before his teammates and Master Wu, looking each of them steadily in the eyes. "I know this is all my fault. But I can still be a true ninja, too. Please. Just give me a second chance. I'll do *anything* to save Ninjago."

Master Wu looked at Lloyd, then turned to the other ninja. "Hmm . . . a true ninja also forgives. Students, are you willing to give Lloyd a second chance?"

"Yes!" Cole, Kai, Nya, and Zane said in unison.

Jay shrugged. "Maybe . . ."

"Then come," Master Wu said seriously. "But know this: Only a true ninja master can complete this journey. If you fail, Ninjago will be lost. And so will all of you . . ."

10

While the ninja set off on their quest for the Ultimate *Ultimate* Weapon, Garmadon's evil gang was busy celebrating their takeover of Ninjago City. Helicopters swarmed above the city's buildings as they transported the volcano top from Garmadon's old headquarters into the city's center.

Garmadon's shark army directed the helicopters' progress.

"A little more," one Sharkman bellowed into his megaphone. "Almost there . . . and stop. Okay, drop it!"

Slowly, the helicopters lowered the volcano top onto the roof of the tower. The volcano erupted in a plume of smoke and lava, officially crowning Garmadon's new lair, Ninjago Tower.

"We did it!" Garmadon's team cheered.

The generals and engineering experts and Sharkmen began partying on the tower's rooftop deck. They went all-out to celebrate this

monumental victory. People leaped into the roof-top pool, chowed down on appetizers, sipped fruity drinks, and congratulated one another. They had been waiting years to celebrate this kind of victory over the ninja.

"Here's a toast to Ninjago's conqueror, Lord Garmadon!" cheered one of the generals.

But Garmadon just couldn't get into the celebration. While everyone else partied, the evil warlord stood alone at the roof's edge, staring out over the vast city — a city he now controlled.

Garmadon watched sadly as the Six-Toed Beast continued to rage around the outskirts of Ninjago City. Even the sight of total destruction couldn't pull him out of his funk. He just kept thinking about what Lloyd had said before he fled: *I wish you weren't my father.*

Garmadon sighed, repeating the words aloud. Quietly, he asked himself, "Is it just me, or was that kind of a weird thing to say? And the tone, it was so disrespectful!"

Suddenly, General Number One stumbled over to Garmadon to offer her congratulations. "Woo-hoo! Nice job conquering!"

"Yeah," agreed General Number Two. "That was *sa-weet!*"

A conga line formed around Lord Garmadon. All the partygoers kicked their feet and chanted, "We conquered Ninjago! We conquered Ninjago! We conquered Ninjago! We conquered Ninjago!"

Garmadon sighed sadly. "Yeah, I know. But what he said — 'I wish you weren't my father.' It's a weird thing, right? I gotta know what he meant by that."

Garmadon shook his head, trying to brush off his bad mood. He snapped to attention suddenly, as though he'd only just noticed the party swirling around him. "General Number One!" he barked.

"Sir!" answered the eye-patch-wearing General Number One.

"Have you captured my son yet?"

"No," the general answered. She took a long sip of her drink. "Not yet, sir."

Garmadon scowled. "Yet here you are, partying on the rooftop with a paper umbrella in your drink."

General Number One chuckled nervously.

"He might be with the others," Garmadon raged on. "What about La-loyd's ninja friends? You captured any of them yet?"

General Number One looked queasy as she muttered, "No, sir."

 73

"Really," Garmadon snapped. "And what about my brother, Wu?"

"Uh, no, sir?" General Number One said, swallowing hard. She didn't like where this line of questioning was going. She took another long sip of her drink, and then held it out to offer her boss a taste.

"What about my ex–old lady? You found her?"

"No," General Number One squeaked. "Sir."

"Well, you certainly had no trouble finding a fruity beverage, did you?" Garmadon howled.

The general hid her drink behind her back. "We're on it, sir," she promised. "We've searched the whole city from top to bottom."

Garmadon took a deep breath and scanned the party. His eyes focused on the entrance to the rooftop patio. He brightened at once when he spotted Koko throwing the door open and striding out onto the patio. She looked furious and, Garmadon thought, lovely as ever.

A bouncer stopped her before she could make her way to Garmadon. "Look, you're not on the list."

Koko knocked the bouncer's clipboard out of his hands and stormed past him, her sights set on her ex.

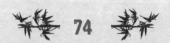

"Well, look at that!" said General Number One. "Here she is now!"

Garmadon growled at General Number One, and then gave a sign to his bodyguards. It was time for a new General Number One. This one was proving to be useless.

As Garmadon gave the nod, General Number One was launched out of the volcano.

Turning to more pleasant matters, Garmadon smiled broadly at his ex-wife. "Hey, Koko! Glad you made it to the party! Pretty on the chain, isn't it?"

"Wipe that smile off your face, Garmadon," Koko spat. "Where's Lloyd? I can't find him anywhere."

"Ugh, you mean the kid that's ruining my conquering party?" Garmadon asked.

"It looks like the Six-Toed Beast is the one conquering the city," Koko said with a smirk. "Not you."

Garmadon rolled his eyes.

"Where is he?" Koko demanded.

"About La-loyd," Garmadon said. "He said the weirdest thing to me . . ."

"Where's Lloyd?" Koko asked again. She shoved him in the chest, nearly pushing him into the pool.

Garmadon windmilled his arms, recovering just in the nick of time.

"Where *is* he? Where's *Lloyd*?" Koko shouted.

All the partygoers watched silently, anticipating the moment their boss blew a fuse. But he didn't. He just blinked, and then smiled patiently at his ex-wife.

"My gosh, woman," he said, his voice filled with warmth. "What happened to us? I miss that fire of yours! I don't know where La-loyd is, but rest assured, I will find him."

Suddenly, one of Garmadon's staff raced across the rooftop deck, crying, "Lord Garmadon! Lord Garmadon! We found him!"

Garmadon grinned at Koko. "See? Gotta go." He and his team of generals strode into the control room. Koko tried to follow, but Garmadon's bodyguards blocked her path.

Inside, a team of experts was studying video monitors and displays. "We've received a report of an old man and six brightly colored suspects heading into the jungle," one of Garmadon's advisors told him.

"There they are!" Garmadon said, peering over his shoulder. "Zoom in a little closer. Closer. *Closer.* No, closer still. Yes! Right in on that kid's lips." He pointed at Kai.

As usual, Kai was chatting away, unaware that

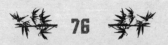

someone very far away was watching his every move.

"What's he saying?" Garmadon asked, staring at the screen intently. "Something about — a weapon? The *Omelette-Omelette Weapon*? Sounds dangerous! Dangerous, yet quite possibly delicious!"

One of the advisors ran the video through their high-tech lip-reading software. "He's talking about an Ultimate *Ultimate* Weapon. Sir."

"That sounds even better than the Ultimate Weapon!" Garmadon said, grinning. "Like, twice as good as the Ultimate Weapon. So that's where I'll find La-loyd. So I can ask him what he meant when he said, 'I wish you weren't my father.' That was weird, right?"

Garmadon didn't wait for a response from his team. He took a deep breath. "I'm going camping!" he declared.

11

Master Wu led the ninja through the dense jungle, across mountaintops, and through rocky passageways. After many hours, the group stopped at the edge of a dense forest. Everyone took a few moments to catch their breath as they scanned the vista before them — dark, towering trees cloaked in mist.

"Students," Master Wu told them, "your training begins now. We are about to enter the Forest of Whispers. Here, you will learn your first ninja skill: silence."

All six ninja leaped into the air, whooping and cheering. "Silence — yeah! All *right*!"

Master Wu shook his head, disappointed. "Unbelievable," he whispered.

The ninja quieted down at once, eager to hear Master Wu's words of wisdom. "Now, you must be as quiet as possible — because this forest is also a *minefield*. And the slightest disturbance could

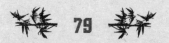

trigger our doom. This is why I did not bring the Fuchsia Ninja."

As soon as Master Wu spoke the words *Fuchsia Ninja*, a crazy ninja in a bright-pink uniform came running toward the group, waving his arms in the air.

Lloyd, Cole, Jay, Kai, Nya, and Zane exchanged confused looks.

"Hey, guys!" the new ninja hollered out. "Don't forget me! Let's do this! Fuchsia Ninja for the —"

KA-BOOM!

A land mine exploded on the forest floor, blasting the Fuchsia Ninja out of the forest and straight back to Ninjago City.

As he flew through the air, the Fuchsia Ninja hollered, "— winnnnnnnnn!"

The other ninja all turned back to Master Wu, terrified and silent.

"Okay," Lloyd said quietly but firmly to his teammates, "we *really* need to listen to Master Wu, guys."

"Totally agree," Nya said, nodding. "One hundred percent."

Jay bobbed his head up and down. "Whatever you think the best way to *not* get land-mined is, I'm fully on board."

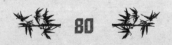

Zane agreed. "Going into 'silent mode' now."

"Good," Master Wu said seriously. "Because embracing your ninjanuity is the only way you will survive this journey." He took a deep breath. "But just in case you don't, I need you to sign these contracts absolving me of any and all legal liability."

Master Wu clicked a button on his flute, turning it into a pen. He handed the pen and a stack of contracts to his students, waiting as they signed the documents.

As soon as they'd finished, the ninja followed him into the forest.

"Hut-hut-hut-hut-hut," they chanted as they marched. "Hut-hut-hut-hut-hut!"

"Shhh!" Master Wu scolded. "Ninja! Silence, remember?"

The ninja mumbled a few complaints before quietly resuming their chant in a whisper. *"Hut-hut-hut-hut-hut-hut."*

"Ugh," Master Wu groaned. "You are all totally gonna get land-mined."

As they continued their quest for the Ultimate *Ultimate* Weapon, the Secret Ninja Force had no

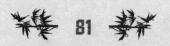

idea that Garmadon was on a similar path nearby in the jungle.

As he pushed through dense foliage, the evil warlord continued brooding over his son's words. "I mean, it's weird," he muttered to himself. He casually swatted a bear out of his way with a back-hand punch. "Just a weird thing to say."

Garmadon stopped in front of a tree, staring at the rough bark. "'I wish you weren't my father,'" he repeated. "'I wish you weren't my FATHER!'"

In a burst of anger, Garmadon karate-chopped the tree. It cracked in half and tumbled to the ground.

"Yeah, Garmadon! Tree slayer." He slumped onto the tree's jagged stump and dropped his face into one hand. "I mean seriously," he grum-bled. "Who wouldn't want me for a dad? I'm awesome."

Suddenly, Garmadon noticed fresh tracks in the dirt nearby. "Wait a minute . . . those are ninja tracks!"

The Secret Ninja Force — whose identities weren't exactly secret anymore — were nearby. Of that he had no doubt. "I smell desperation," Garmadon cheered. He jumped up and followed the footprints through the forest.

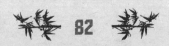

It didn't take long for him to find the ninja. When he sensed that he was very close, Garmadon slowed his progress. He knew the element of surprise would give him an advantage. The ninja clearly had no idea he was coming after them.

On the other side of a grove of trees, Master Wu suddenly slowed down and took a deep breath in.

"Hmmm . . ." he said, sniffing left and then right. "I smell evil."

Leaving the ninja behind, Wu somersaulted in midair, and then karate-chopped his way into a bamboo grove. He spun and whirled through the forest. Moments later, he found himself face-to-face with his brother.

Garmadon stared at Wu.

Wu glared at Garmadon.

Then they both narrowed their eyes and hissed, "You!"

The brothers continued their stare-down for a few long, tense moments. Finally, Garmadon broke the silence. "Hello, brother." He gritted his teeth. "Why did you turn La-loyd against me?"

"Me?" Master Wu scoffed. "I didn't turn him against you. *You* turned him against you."

"I'm not here to fight you," Garmadon said. "I

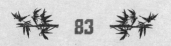

just need to talk to La-loyd. Oh, and take the Ultimate *Ultimate* Weapon."

Just then, Lloyd rushed into the clearing. The other ninja weren't far behind.

"Oh, hey, La-loyd!" Garmadon said, waving. "Yeah, it's me, Dad! So, I'm just wrapping things up with your weird uncle here."

Garmadon began walking toward Lloyd, but Wu blocked him with his staff.

"I will not let you harm the boy!" Wu said, swinging his staff again. "And I will *not* let you take the Ultimate *Ultimate* Weapon!" He launched into a series of smoothly executed martial-arts moves. He swung his flute at his brother, but Garmadon pivoted out of the way.

"Ha-ha!" Garmadon cackled. "The old 'Swinging Flute' move? So predictable . . ."

Garmadon leaped over Wu, landing gracefully on his other side. "How about a 'Swinging Bamboo Kick'?" he shouted. He swung through the air on a bamboo shoot, aiming his feet at Master Wu's face.

Wu effortlessly stepped out of the way.

Garmadon and Wu stared at each other for a moment. Then they leaped into the air, spinning and kicking at each other inside the dense bamboo forest.

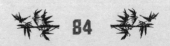

Wu slashed at his brother with his staff, but Garmadon managed to bob and weave to escape his blows. It was clear that the two brothers were evenly matched.

Finally, Garmadon landed a strike that knocked Wu's hat off his head. He flipped it onto his own head, grinning wickedly at his brother.

"Hey!" Master Wu said, rushing toward him. "My hat!"

Both men jumped at each other, punching and kicking and launching fierce attacks.

Lloyd watched helplessly, wishing he could do something to stop the fight. But Wu and Garmadon were in their own world — it was a fight they'd been waiting to have for many years. A fight they had to fight alone.

"How about the 'Block of Seagulls,' brother?" Wu taunted. He punched and then cried, "Time for 'Crouching Monkey, Angry Rooster'!"

Garmadon launched himself into the air and roared, "This move's called the 'Sky Fall'!"

Wu and Garmadon crashed to the ground. They began tumbling down a steep embankment, rolling past the ninja.

Lloyd hurried after his father and uncle, telling his teammates, "Wu's fighting Garmadon! It's an

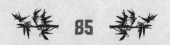

epic grudge match! This way!" He raced down the cliff, pausing briefly when he and the other ninja reached a rickety rope bridge.

The bridge swayed under the weight of the fighting brothers. Garmadon continued throwing punches, while Wu swung his staff to block the blows.

"How about this one?" Master Wu grunted. He began knocking planks of wood off the bridge with his flute. The planks flew through the air, whacking Garmadon in the face. "I call it the 'Meatloaf Surprise'!"

Wu grabbed Garmadon and smashed him through the wooden planks of the bridge — sending him spiraling toward the ground far, far below.

"Oh my gosh!" Lloyd gasped when he realized Garmadon was dangling upside down by his feet from the underside of the bridge. He'd stopped his fall! "Master Wu — look down!"

"You're still using that old move?" Wu said, unimpressed by Garmadon's balancing act.

"Bet you've never seen this one," Garmadon said, chuckling. He wound his body up inside the bridge rope, spun, and then launched himself high

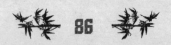

into the air. He flipped in midair, landing with two feet on the far side of the bridge.

Garmadon let out a satisfied chuckle. He had always been sure he was a better fighter than his wimpy brother. "I call it 'The Untitled Garmadon Project'!"

"How about this one?" Wu countered. He back-flipped away while simultaneously hurling a wave of bamboo sticks at his brother.

Garmadon tried to duck out of the way, but it was too late. A huge bamboo cage dropped down from the tree above him. It landed on the bridge, trapping Garmadon inside.

The evil warlord groaned.

"I call it the 'Caged Idiot,'" Master Wu said, smirking.

"Oh, you have *got* to be kidding me," Garmadon roared.

Wu chuckled happily. He smiled at the ninja, who were watching the battle between brothers in awe. "And that, my students, is how you fight like a true ninja — *WHOA!*"

A butterfly fluttered out of nowhere and landed on Master Wu's nose. Wu brushed at his face. As he did, his foot slipped on the rickety bridge. A

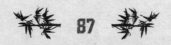

moment later, he'd lost his balance and stumbled backward.

It all happened so fast, the ninja had no time to react. They just watched helplessly as Master Wu toppled off the side of the bridge, twisted and turned in the air, and tumbled toward the rushing river below.

Master Wu was gone.

12

ncle Wu!" Lloyd screamed.

"A *butterfly* made him fall off a bridge?!" Jay cried, staring at the spot where Master Wu had been standing just moments before.

The ninja peered over the edge of the rope bridge, hoping for some sign that their master had survived the fall.

Seconds later, Master Wu's head popped up out of the frothing water. The ninja heard him calling out to them. "Ninja! There's only one thing to remember. It's most important that you — *AHH!*"

The water swept him downstream, and Wu was gone.

"Uncle Wu!" Lloyd cried. "What's important?"

"What do we do?" Nya yelled.

"Don't leave us alone," Jay said, glancing around at the scary forest.

"Uncle Wu!" Lloyd howled.

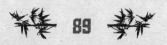

"Guys, we can't do it," Jay said finally. "Without Master Wu, we're done for."

Zane nodded. "According to my calculations, our chances of survival without a ninja master are . . . zero point zero, zero, zero."

"Great, we got it," Nya snapped. "Thanks, Zane."

"I'm gonna throw up!" Jay wailed.

"So, your master's gone," Garmadon said musingly. "If you want to survive the journey that lies ahead, you're gonna need a ninja master. Which I just happen to be. In fact, I'm even better. I'm a ninja WARLORD."

Garmadon began hissing at the ninja. He wiggled his arms in the air. Then he flicked his serpent tongue.

The ninja all took a step back. Even safely inside a cage, Garmadon was terrifying.

"Now," Garmadon went on, "do you seriously think this dinky little dog carrier is going to hold Lord Garmadon?"

He punched at one of the bars on his cage. It didn't budge.

Garmadon shook the bars. Nothing.

Then he rammed his body against the bamboo cage. Still nothing.

Garmadon grunted and pushed, but the cage was obviously very solid.

"Guys, what do we do?" Lloyd asked. "Bring him with us?"

"How is that good?" Jay screeched. "That's the opposite of good!"

"But Garmadon did make some solid points about how we'll never survive on our own," Cole said.

"We do need a ninja master," Zane agreed.

"I say we leave him here to rot," Kai said.

Nya shook her head. "Whoa, whoa, whoa, *whoa*. This is *Garmadon* we're talking about. Let me paint a picture for you: What if some local yokel out chopping wood — with an axe! — comes by and lets Garmadon go free? He just chops a nice big hole in the side of the cage and then Garmadon goes on his merry way?"

The ninja all considered this for a moment. Nya had a point. If they left Garmadon alone in the woods, there was a decent chance he would find a way to get free. But if they dragged him along, they could keep an eye on him to make sure he couldn't do any more damage.

"We take him," Lloyd said, sighing.

13

The journey through the forest was much more difficult without Wu along to guide them. And it was considerably more draining with Garmadon's cage in tow. The ninja took turns pulling and pushing the extra weight, but no one was happy to have their prisoner along for the ride.

"You kids are gonna need my dark ninja skills," Garmadon said as they struggled to haul the cage over a hilltop. "Doing this thing warlord style is the only way you're going to stay alive."

"I'm not doing anything warlord style," Lloyd muttered. "Because I'll never be a warlord."

Garmadon rolled his eyes. "Not with *that* attitude you won't."

The ninja made their way down into a ravine. They soon realized it was considerably easier to carry the cage *downhill* than it was going up.

"Wait a minute," Garmadon said, peering out of

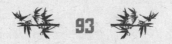

his cage at the dark valley below. "A dark ravine? I wouldn't go in there, and I'm Lord Garmadon! Here's a warlord pro-tip: Never give the high ground to your enemy."

"But . . ." Jay said, "*you're* our enemy."

"You know what?" Garmadon said. "Fine. Good luck in Ambush City. Keep your eyes peeled, because woods like these are full of thieves, bandits —"

Lloyd cut his dad off. "Keep moving. Ignore him."

Hours later, the ninja stumbled across a makeshift camp deep inside the forest. The clearing was untidy, with old appliances and junk scattered across the forest floor.

As the ninja approached, they could see a man in the distance. He was wearing a filthy tool belt and he was covered in tattoos. He appeared to be meditating atop a huge boulder in the center of the ravine.

"Ohhhhhhhhmmmmmmmmm," the man hummed. "Ohhhhhhhhmmmmmmmmm."

The ninja tried to slip past the man unnoticed. But the man called out, "Bup-bup-bup-bup-bup. I

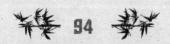

am Quan, and this is Quan's pass. You want to pass through here, you have to pay the toll."

"We didn't bring any money with us," Zane said.

"No pockets," Jay said, shrugging. "That's the problem with ninja pants."

"What are you *doing*?" Garmadon whispered furiously. "Don't negotiate with this guy! You just pick up that rock and smash him in the head."

Lloyd shushed him. "Okay, let me handle this, please?!"

Quan considered the group. He surveyed each of them, and then finally said, "I'll take . . . the pretty boy's silk scarf."

Jay gasped. "What?! My mother gave me this scarf." He wrapped his hands around his scarf protectively.

"Jay, come on," Kai urged. "Just give him the scarf!"

"Ho-ho!" Quan cried out. "You wanna tussle?" He jumped off the boulder.

When he landed next to them, the ninja realized Quan was *tiny*.

"Aww," Nya cooed. "Look at how little he is! He's so cute."

Jay giggled. "I just want to pat him on his little head."

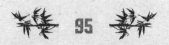

"Do it," Garmadon hissed. "With a rock."

Quan heaved a sigh, and then the little man tapped the side of the boulder.

A moment later, the boulder blinked open. It was a giant eye!

Quan began to assemble a bunch of spare parts, and within seconds, the eye was tottering on top of two huge legs and a body with a single arm wielding a battle axe.

"Ninja," Quan said, grinning evilly. "Meet Gary. Gary — GET NINJA!"

"All right," Garmadon said, whooping as he saw that they finally had a worthy adversary. "Time to conquer this bad boy. Who's with me?"

As Cyclops Gary rushed toward them, the Secret Ninja Force panicked. "Ahhhhh!" they screamed, scattering in different directions as Gary's enormous arm came crashing down at them.

"Didn't Wu teach you *any* moves?" Garmadon groaned as the ninja hurried out of harm's way.

"We don't know anything!" the ninja screamed.
BOOM!

Another blow narrowly missed the ninja. Parts flew off the huge cyclops body as he smashed his fists into the ground over and over again.

"Ow! My hand!" Cyclops Gary moaned.

Quan stood to the side, furiously rebuilding his cyclops friend. He swiftly reconstructed Gary's hand, and then attached it and gave his pal a high five.

Gary was back in business. He tried to stomp a fleeing ninja, but his foot flew off.

"Footsie!" Gary wailed.

Quan quickly rebuilt Gary's foot, while Lloyd swooped in and grabbed Gary's battle axe off the forest floor.

"La-loyd!" Garmadon yelled. "Let me out of the cage! Hurry!"

Lloyd looked at his father, considering. With the evil warlord's help, they could easily defeat Gary.

Garmadon pressed his advantage. "I can teach you the 'Soul-Eater,' the 'Buzz Kill,' the 'Dance of Death' . . . we can take this guy!"

"I — I —" Lloyd stammered. "I just — I don't —"

Suddenly, Gary plucked Lloyd off the ground and dangled him in the air.

"Come on!" Garmadon called out. Then his eyes widened as he realized he'd captured Gary's attention.

Gary stormed toward the cage, and Garmadon backed away from the bars. "Oh, boy . . . here we go."

Gary ripped off the top of Garmadon's cage

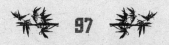 97

and jammed Lloyd in beside his father. Then he cinched the top of the cage back together with a length of vine.

Realizing that the only way to help Lloyd was to *not* get caught, the rest of the ninja fled the campsite.

"What *is* that thing?" Kai asked, turning back to look at Gary.

"What are we gonna do?" Jay asked.

They sprinted around a corner, their sights set on a hollow log spanning a deep ravine. The ninja dove into the log, hoping that they could shimmy through it and reach the other side of the ravine before Gary caught them.

"Terror levels increasing," Zane said as he and the other ninja scurried through the log.

Suddenly, the log tilted. The ninja braced themselves as they felt the log lifting and shifting into the air. When they glanced back in the direction they had come from, the ninja realized Gary had lifted the log right off the ground!

The giant cyclops squinted into the log, checking to make sure he'd found the ninja. He gave the log a vigorous shake, but the ninja held tight.

Cyclops Gary lifted the log to his mouth. Then he inhaled.

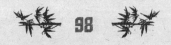

Quan raced around the corner and cried, "No! Don't blow it!"

But it was too late. Before Quan could stop him, Cyclops Gary blew the log like a horn.

The ninja went flying in different directions. With one massive exhale, Gary had scattered them throughout the jungle.

"Too bad," Quan said. "I really liked that scarf."

Shrugging, he gestured to his friend. "Come on, Gary. Let's get back to camp."

"Okay, Poppy," Gary said. With a blink of his enormous eye, the giant creature trailed along after Quan, dragging the cage with Garmadon and Lloyd behind him.

99

14

A hh," Garmadon said, relaxing back against the bars of the cage.

It was later that night. He and Lloyd were on full display in the center of Gary and Quan's camp. The only silver lining to their situation was that the cage was situated next to the campfire, so they weren't likely to freeze. "Is there anything better than a campfire on a cold night? This is nice, isn't it?"

Lloyd glared at him. Then he turned away and sniffled.

Garmadon shook his head sadly, studying his son's face in the firelight. "La-loyd, are you crying? 'Cause warlords don't cry. And if we did, we'd cry tears of fire."

"I'm not crying," Lloyd said. "I just want to get out of this cage so I can find my friends and save Ninjago City."

"So," Garmadon said, looking at Lloyd seriously.

"Speaking of Ninjago City . . . was there something you said to me back there? Can't remember what it was exactly . . ."

"I wish you weren't my father," Lloyd snapped.

"Was that it?" Garmadon said lightly. "I really wasn't listening. But I thought maybe you'd like to, I don't know . . . *un*-say it?"

Lloyd shook his head and turned to look at him. "Look, Garmadon —"

"Dad," Garmadon corrected. "You can call me Dad. Or Super-Awesome All-Powerful Warlord. That works, too."

"Look, *Garmadon*," Lloyd said. "You know why I said that to you? Because you make my life miserable. Every day, people ignore me, kids make fun of me —"

Garmadon cut him off. "Whoa, whoa, whoa. Hold on. Somebody's picking on you? Then stand up for yourself and shoot them out of a volcano! That's how I roll. Problem solved."

"Yeah," Lloyd grumbled.

"You gotta get yourself a volcano, kid," Garmadon told him.

"Hey!" Quan's voice rang out from across the campsite.

Garmadon and Lloyd both looked up.

"Can you please keep your dysfunctional relationship down?" Quan called. "We can't hear the TV."

In the silence that followed, Lloyd and Garmadon could hear a news report blaring out of the TV. "Stay tuned for a *special report*!" a newscaster announced. "Disaster has struck in Ninjago City."

Lloyd craned his neck, trying to see the images on the small screen. Garmadon scrambled to his feet and stood next to him. They both peered through the bars of their cage. If they put their heads close together, they could each see one corner of the screen.

Lloyd and his dad watched together as the Six-Toed Beast hit Garmadon's volcano, knocking it off the top of Ninjago Tower. Then a familiar face flashed across the screen — Koko! She flinched, and then raced out of the way of falling debris.

"Mom?" Lloyd said quietly, desperately.

"My volcano!" Garmadon cried.

He and Lloyd exchanged a long look.

"We need to get that Ultimate *Ultimate* Weapon," Garmadon said.

"How are we gonna do that?" Lloyd asked.

"Remember those three-legged races you and I never did when you were a kid?" Garmadon asked.

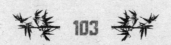

"Um —" Lloyd began.

"This is gonna be just like that wasn't," Garmadon explained.

They waited until Quan and Cyclops Gary were engrossed in their favorite TV show. Then Garmadon and Lloyd gently tipped their cage onto its side. Carefully, they poked their legs out of the bars and stepped forward.

The cage teetered, tottered, and spun in circles.

"Wait," Lloyd whispered. "We've got to get in sync. You hear that song on the TV? That's our tempo. Left, right, left, right."

Garmadon chimed in, "Left, right, left, right, left, right . . ."

They began to walk to the beat, and within a few minutes, their cage had vanished into the jungle.

But before long, the pair lost their rhythm. "Left, right — *falllllll!*" They'd stepped right off a steep hill!

When they heard the father-and-son cry echoing through the forest, Gary and Quan leaped up from their seats. They glanced across the campsite and realized that Garmadon and Lloyd were gone.

Gary howled in rage. He hoisted Quan onto his shoulder. They raced through the forest after their prisoners.

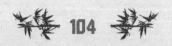

Deep in the forest, Garmadon and Lloyd rolled downhill. At the bottom, they bounced over rocks and flew into the air. They finally landed in a crevice at the bottom of the embankment.

Working together, Garmadon and Lloyd tried to get free. But they were wedged in tight. No matter how hard they shook the bars of their cage, it was clear they weren't going anywhere. They were stuck.

Just then, Cyclops Gary appeared on the crest of the hill above them. He roared furiously as he leaped through the air after his prisoners. Gary landed atop the cage with a thunderous crash — knocking it free!

Now Gary was wedged in the crevice. The giant cyclops was stuck, and his prisoners, still caged, were on the loose.

Gary let out a howl of misery as Garmadon and Lloyd raced away.

15

An hour later, Garmadon and Lloyd burst through a curtain of dense jungle growth. They were still in the cage, but they'd finally gotten their steps back in sync. Now they found themselves in a shadowy, spooky clearing.

As soon as his eyes adjusted to the dim light, Lloyd noticed a few shadowy figures creeping toward them.

Garmadon muttered, "Oh," just as Gary and Quan rushed out of the forest behind them.

"Uh-oh," Lloyd said, trying to scramble away.

"Who have you got in your cage, highwayman?" the shadowy figure asked Quan.

"We found a *red-eyed, four-armed weirdo* and his disrespectful son in the jungle," Quan replied.

The figure leaned forward, peering into the darkness of the cage. "Red eyes . . . four arms . . ."

The shadowy figure stepped into the light. A golden star flashed on his chest. It was the shark-headed general, the guy Garmadon had shot out of his volcano earlier that day!

"Garmadon," the general said. His tone was unreadable.

"General Number One!" Garmadon said, obviously relieved to see a familiar face. He stretched his legs, excited that someone would *finally* be able to help him get out of this cage. Garmadon chuckled. A trusty employee certainly was a *fine* sight for sore eyes.

"Well, well, well," the shark-headed general said, studying the two prisoners. "I'll bet you're surprised to see me."

"Yeah!" Garmadon said happily. "Surprised and delighted." He snapped into boss mode. "Okay, General! Get me out of this cage. Then let's see about getting me some lunch. I'm starving."

The shark-headed general didn't move a muscle. He just stared Garmadon down, as though he hadn't heard his command.

"That's an *order*, General Number One," Garmadon told him in his bossiest boss voice.

There was a long, tense silence. Then more figures stepped out of the shadows. Their crazed

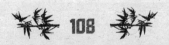

laughter combined with the sounds of the wild animal calls of the jungle, filling the air with creepy cackling.

"Isn't that rich?" the general said, trying to catch his breath. "An order?! You can't give me orders. You . . . fired . . . me . . . !!"

The general drew a dagger and waved it in front of Garmadon. Lloyd flinched as Garmadon backed away from the bars of the cage.

Suddenly, another one of Garmadon's former General Number Ones stepped out of the shadows. It was the eye-patch general, the same one Garmadon had fired after Lloyd had unleashed the Ultimate Weapon.

Eye-Patch General Number One adjusted her patch, and then took a long slurp out of her beverage. "What he was going to say is, you *fired* us . . . out of a volcano!" She whipped out a red-hot sword and waved it under Garmadon's nose.

Hundreds of Garmadon's former employees emerged from the shadows. And it seemed that all of them had, at one time, been Garmadon's General Number One.

Garmadon gulped nervously as crowds of his former generals swarmed the cage, lifted it into the air, and carried it away.

"Come on, Gary. Let's watch!" Quan said. He and Cyclops Gary chased after the group.

As they trekked through the jungle, the generals all seemed a little crazed — wild-eyed, angry, and slightly charred (probably from the volcano). They leaped and jumped in front of Garmadon, poking at him through the bars with their spears.

As Lloyd and Garmadon's cage was hoisted up and carried along, more generals swung past them on vines.

"You sure fired a lot of generals," Lloyd said quietly.

Garmadon shrugged. "Yeah, I could never find the perfect General Number One. Not for lack of trying, either."

As Garmadon batted away spears, he noticed the angry looks on the faces surrounding the cage. He had a sinking suspicion he could forget about getting a sandwich. "Got any more drinks out there?" he asked the eye-patch general with a hopeful smile. "I'm parched."

16

Hey! Jay!" Nya waved her arms, trying to get her fellow ninja's attention. After trudging through the jungle alone for hours, Nya was relieved to see one of her teammates behind a wall of bamboo.

Jay stepped out of a bamboo maze and waved back at Nya.

A moment later, Cole, Kai, and Zane emerged from the jungle, too. They were all hot and sweaty, and they looked very ragged.

"Dude," Cole said, cringing when he saw Kai. The Red Ninja had lost his gi somewhere within the jungle. All Kai had on was his underwear and one dirty sock.

"Not a good look, bro," Nya told her brother.

"Oh, man!" Kai gasped, staring wild-eyed at his friends. "I was starting to think I'd never see a living person again! I mean, this jungle is ruthless!"

111

"I know," Jay agreed. "I almost died multiple times."

Nya held up a hand. "Hold on. None of us *did* die, though. How did that happen?"

Cole shrugged. "Well, I disguised myself as a bush."

"I was frozen in fear. I stayed perfectly still," Jay said.

"I heard a loud noise and turned down my volume knob," Zane added.

"I took off my gi," said Kai.

"And then what?" Nya asked.

"That's it," Kai said. "I just took off my gi."

"Okay," Nya said. "That is less helpful." She took a deep breath, considering her next words carefully.

Nya had had a lot of time to think during her hours alone in the jungle, and she'd had a burst of inspiration. "Listen, guys, this is just like Master Wu was trying to teach us. We didn't need our mechs to survive. We were invisible. We were one with the elements. We were silent ... but deadly."

There was a long pause.

"Whoa," Cole said seriously. "None of us laughed this time."

"We're ready," the ninja said together.

"What do you say we find Lloyd, get that Ultimate *Ultimate* Weapon, and save Ninjago?" Nya asked.

The others cheered. "*NINJA-GO!*"

Nya nodded. Then she turned to her brother again. "But, Kai? Put some pants on first."

Kai grinned, giving her a cheeky thumbs-up.

The ninja set off again through the jungle forest. It was time to dig deep and become ninja. The fate of Ninjago — and the fate of their friend — was in their hands.

Cole, Jay, Kai, Nya, and Zane had been walking purposefully for quite a while when Cole stopped suddenly to examine a broken tree branch. He rubbed its lone leaf. Then he sniffed it, considering.

Nya reached forward and plucked a single thread off the tree, studying it.

Kai bent down and licked a cluster of footprints on the ground.

Zane's eyes glowed as he scanned the surroundings with a beam of light. "Lloyd is nearby," he told the others, "and in considerable danger."

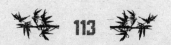

Back at the generals' camp, Lloyd was growing more and more irritated by the moment. He rattled around inside the cage as a group of generals marched them along. The group was carrying torches and chanting,

Hold your head up, hold it high!
Generals are marching by!
We've got Gar-ma-don and son!
He has lost and we have won.

"Fine! Sing your songs and do your worst," Garmadon hollered through the bars of their cage. "I'd fire you all again in a heartbeat. A heartbeat!" He looked at Lloyd and shook his head. "You know what? I've learned something tonight."

Lloyd sighed. "That you really need an HR department?"

Garmadon ignored him. "I've learned that people don't love you just because you command them to. Which is weird —"

"You're right," Lloyd said angrily. "They don't. It's not that easy."

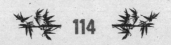

He looked at his father and wished, not for the first time, that things could be different between the two of them.

Just as Lloyd began to wonder if, maybe, it wasn't too late to fix things, a horn blared in the distance.

"Looks like we're finally leaving the Valley of Madness," Garmadon said, pointing. "And going straight to Crazytown."

Lloyd glanced up. Letters scrawled across a huge, ancient wall read: "Crazytown."

One of the generals blew a horn, and a gate in the wall swung open. Lloyd and Garmadon peered out of their cage, trying to figure out what was happening.

With a loud cheer, a crowd of excited generals parted to reveal an artificial volcano that had been built on one side of the village.

"It's an exact reproduction of your old volcanic lair!" Eye-Patch General Number One informed Garmadon. "One-quarter scale."

"Oh, how nice," Garmadon said loftily. "What a flattering tribute."

"Oh, yeah," the general replied, snickering as she slurped up the last drops of her fruity drink. "We're gonna *fire* you out of it."

Garmadon's face fell. What traitors! What treachery!

"General Number One!" the eye-patch general barked.

"Yes, General Number One?" someone called back.

The eye-patch general grinned at Lloyd and Garmadon. Then she hollered, "Take them to the top!"

17

Lloyd held tightly to the bars of the cage as a mechanical crane lifted the bamboo prison up into the air. He and Garmadon were hefted onto a platform near the mouth of the volcano.

Deep inside the village, one of Garmadon's former General Number Ones beat on a large kettledrum as another group of generals heaved a gigantic charcoal briquette into the center of the volcano.

With a smug grin, the eye-patch general struck a wooden matchstick and tossed the flame into the volcano. She performed a quick fire dance, and the volcano blazed to life. Fire and embers shot out of the volcano's core, and everyone cheered.

Someone began to chant, "Fire him! Fire him! Fire him!" Soon, all the generals were chanting along.

 117

Angry mobs of fired generals used long sticks to push the cage closer and closer to the mouth of the red-hot volcano. They jeered and whooped as the cage tottered near the edge of the platform.

"Ooh, boy," Garmadon said, wiping sweat off his face.

Lloyd took a deep breath. This was the end. He was doomed, all because of his terrible father. It figured.

Unbeknownst to Lloyd, the other ninja had just slipped into the generals' camp, and they were preparing to rescue him.

"Okay, guys," Nya said quietly as they joined the back of the crowd. "If we're gonna free Lloyd, we need to use our ninja skills: camouflage, silence, and misdirection."

"I'll use the ninja skill of stealth karate chops to take these guys down . . . silently!" Kai slashed his hand through the air, taking down a few generals who had been lurking at the back of the mob.

"I'll use the ninja skill of ultimate disguise," Cole said, "to be disguised." He pulled the helmets off some of Garmadon's former generals, and then he and the other ninja slipped them onto their own heads. They were now disguised and could blend in perfectly. Sneaky, like ninja!

"I'll use the ninja skill of stand-up comedy," Zane said, deadpan. He slipped a fishbowl helmet over his ninja mask.

"Zane," Nya said, stopping. "What?"

Just as Lloyd was coming to terms with the fact that he'd reached the end, he heard a familiar voice call out, "Good evening, ladies and generals! Are you all . . . *FIRED UP*?!"

The generals spun around, searching for the source of the voice in the shadows at the back of the crowd. Zane had managed to draw all attention to himself.

"Ah," Jay said, realizing what Zane had planned. "Ninja misdirection. Got it."

As Zane told silly jokes to keep the generals busy, the other ninja crept toward Lloyd's cage. No one, not even Lloyd, noticed them sneaking across the platform. No one spotted them weaving through the crowd. They had finally managed to do just what Master Wu was always telling them to do — move with stealth and speed. They slipped past everyone without being noticed. *Totally* ninja.

"Lloyd," Nya whispered, suddenly right beside him. "We're here to rescue you!" She pried at the knot that was holding the door of the cage closed.

"Wow, ninja," Garmadon whispered back. "I'm touched."

"Oh, umm," Cole said. "The thing is . . . we're only here for Lloyd."

"Oh," Garmadon said, surprised. "Look, your ninja skills may have gotten you up to here, but only the sick skills of a conquering warlord can save you now."

Lloyd wiped sweat off his brow. He glanced down at the crowd gathered below, and then stole a glance at the generals hovering nearby on the platform.

"Guys," Lloyd said, glancing at his father. "Do it." He motioned for Nya to untie the knot. Reluctantly, Nya slid the knot loose.

"Oh, you won't regret it," Garmadon said, grinning wickedly. "Just wait until you see your old man in action, La-loyd!"

Garmadon stepped out of the cage. "Uh, excuse me," he said, tapping one of the generals on the shoulder. "General Number One?"

"Yes?" the generals all replied in unison.

Garmadon launched into a spinning attack that sent the generals flying like bowling pins. They spilled off the edges of the platform.

"Fore!" he called, tossing a general high into the air. Garmadon cackled as the generals around him fell away one by one.

Suddenly, the village horn sounded again, and dozens more generals came swarming forward. Cyclops Gary and Quan were among them.

"Oh . . ." Garmadon said, wincing a little when he realized what he and the ninja were up against.

"Listen," Lloyd told the others. "If you guys can hold them off, I can build something to get us out of here. But I'm gonna need bricks."

"On it!" Garmadon said, snapping to attention. He looked at the rest of the ninja. "You kids ready to learn the 'Dance of Death'? This is essential warlording stuff."

"Oh, we are so ready!" Nya said.

"Oh, yeah?" Garmadon said, skeptical.

"Oh, yeah!" Nya said.

As the angry mob of generals climbed up the side of the volcano toward the ninja, Garmadon called out, "All right, then — hit it!"

In a flash, the platform turned into a colorfully lit dance floor. Garmadon jumped and spun, calling out, "*You just . . . jump up! Kick back! Whip around and spin.*" He executed a series of moves

121

that were part dancing, part fighting. "*Then you . . . jump back. Kick front! Do it all again!*"

The ninja sang along, "*Jump back! Kick front! Do it all again!*"

Nya spun and kicked, hollering, "Hey, Garmadon, I hope you're ready for this dance." She and the other ninja performed their moves perfectly. Generals went sailing through the air as Lloyd, Cole, Jay, Kai, Nya, and Zane joined Garmadon's dance offensive.

"Yeah!" Garmadon cheered, dancing left and right to avoid the mighty swings of Cyclops Gary. "Do it!"

Lord Garmadon punched Cyclops Gary, sending his head hurling through the air. Then Garmadon grabbed the giant creature by the arm and flipped him over — sending spare parts and pieces flying. Garmadon passed the pieces to Lloyd, who began to build something new out of Gary's spare parts.

As the rest of the ninja spun and kicked and sent pieces of the generals flying through the air, Lloyd continued gathering stray bricks and pieces. He built as fast as he could. He knew just what he needed to do to get them out of the jungle and back to Ninjago to save their city.

"Build it!" Garmadon said encouragingly. He tossed more loose bricks toward Lloyd.

"Yes!" Lloyd said, grinning.

Lloyd continued to build until his creation was almost complete. Finally, he slammed the last piece on top and studied his creation: It was the perfect getaway helicopter!

"Oh, boy! Let's go," Garmadon said, urging the others to hurry as dozens more generals encircled the group.

Garmadon hopped into the helicopter. Lloyd settled in next to him, taking up the controls. The rest of the ninja piled into the back.

The helicopter lifted up and sailed over the treetops. It bucked and pitched wildly in the high winds, but at least they'd finally escaped the angry mob of fired generals.

"Whoa, whoa, whoa," Garmadon said, reaching across Lloyd for the controls. "Let me teach you how to drive this thing."

Lloyd gave him a long look. "I drive mechs. I think I can handle this."

"Oh, good," Garmadon said. "Good. But just in case, put your hands on ten and two." He leaned over and showed Lloyd what he meant. "Steady . . ."

Lloyd pointed ahead. "Guys, look! It's the temple Master Wu told us about. It's just ahead!"

"All right, watch your speed, La-loyd. Don't grind the gears," Garmadon instructed.

"Okay, okay," Lloyd said, grinning. "I've got it. Got it!"

"You're doing great," Garmadon told him.

But suddenly, a goat perched on top of a mountain emerged out of the mist. The helicopter was heading straight for it!

Lloyd swerved, but the helicopter clipped the side of the mountain, then rocked and slanted wildly. Garmadon and the ninja held on for dear life as they tilted and spun through the air.

The helicopter plummeted toward Temple Mountain, where it slammed onto a slope and skidded to a stop.

"Is everyone okay?" Lloyd asked as he climbed out of the makeshift helicopter.

"Not really," Jay grumbled, brushing himself off.

Everyone was a little banged up, but no one was seriously hurt.

"Behold . . ." Garmadon said, pointing through the mist. "The Temple of Fragile Foundations."

18

O kay," Garmadon said as they approached the temple. "Be cool, be stealthy. Any loud noise could trigger an avalanche."

The ninja all exchanged worried glances.

An avalanche? Lloyd wondered. Was Garmadon being serious?

Two sculpted guard dogs flanked either side of the temple's entrance, offering visitors a grim, sinister welcome.

Kai reached out and pulled a handful of air to his face. "I sense bad memories," he said sadly.

"Terrible loneliness," Nya agreed.

"Gloomy angst and desperation," Cole said.

Garmadon shrugged. "Well, I've spent a lot of time here and believe me ... it doesn't get any better."

"Wait a minute," Lloyd said as they stepped up to the temple door. "So you know this place?"

Garmadon brushed years-old dust and cobwebs away from a doormat labeled: "The Garmadons." He gazed down at it sadly. "Who doesn't know . . . their childhood home?"

Everyone looked at him, startled. *This* was where Wu and Garmadon had grown up?

As if in answer to their unspoken question, Garmadon bent down and lifted up the doormat. Underneath it was a key.

Garmadon picked it up and turned it in the lock. "Yeah. This place is so unstable I had to move to a volcano just to feel safe. Well — shall we?"

The door creaked, swinging open to reveal a pitch-black hallway. The light from outside fought the gloom, casting strange, creepy shadows across the dark floor.

"This is my least favorite place I've ever been," Jay said. He shuddered with each step he took inside the massive temple. He touched the wall near the front door. "Oh, look! A light switch," he said happily, flicking it on.

For a long moment, no one said anything as they gazed around the entryway. There was so much to take in.

The interior of the Garmadon house was like a relic from the 1970s. There was nothing holy or

templelike about it — everything about the space was totally unexpected. And totally cheesy.

"Orange shag carpeting?" Jay giggled.

"Ew!" Kai said, pointing. "The sofa has plastic slipcovers."

Garmadon frowned. "We had pets."

"What is *that*?" Cole said, pointing to an over-the-top, old-fashioned living room.

"It's called class," Garmadon said. He was clearly ready to defend his home all day if he had to. "Why don't you get some?"

"Look!" Zane said, racing down a hallway. "Family photos!"

The ninja hurried after him. They oohed and ahhed as they studied old photos of Garmadon and Wu as kids. Master Wu had had a full beard, even as a baby — and Lord Garmadon had only two arms!

"They're so cute," Kai said, cooing.

Lloyd stared at the photos in disbelief, moving along the hallway to look at all the framed memories. He stopped in front of a picture of two people in the middle of a battle.

"That's you," he said, glancing at Garmadon. "And that's . . ." It was Garmadon, fighting side by side with —

"Oh my gosh!" Nya said, her eyes wide. "That's Lady Iron Dragon! My hero!"

"Yes," Garmadon said. "Lady Iron Dragon. Also known as your mom, Lloyd."

"Wait," Lloyd said, shocked, "what? Mom was a *warrior*?"

"Yes," Garmadon replied.

"But she always said she was a defensive strategist," Lloyd argued.

"She was," Garmadon said, shrugging. "Her defensive strategies were legendary. No one could break through them. I remember the first time I saw her . . ."

Garmadon smiled, thinking back to the first time he'd laid eyes on his ex-wife. "It was the Battle of Nine Armies," he went on. "I was in charge of the hostile takeover of Kung Fu-go. I spotted this beautiful warrior queen from across a crowded battlefield." He chuckled, remembering how magnificent Koko had looked in her battle gear. "She was fearless, aggressive, vicious. They called her Lady Iron Dragon, and boy, she was something. I was speechless."

Lloyd held up a hand. "Hold on a second . . . Mom said you met in a copy room."

"I don't even know what that *is*," Garmadon

snapped. He rolled his eyes and went on. "Anyway, as I was saying . . . I was speechless. Her 'Triple Spin Back Kick' intimidated me, but I worked up the nerve and I approached her. I asked her if she fought here often." Garmadon giggled, thinking back to his clever pick-up line. "She said . . . she *did*."

Lloyd stared at his father in shock. How was it possible his parents had such different versions of this story?! And his mom had been . . . a *warrior*?

"I don't know," Garmadon said, caught up in his memories. "There was just something about her. We . . . clicked. It was like we could read each other's thoughts. We were perfectly matched. It was love at first fight!"

Lloyd narrowed his eyes. "Wait a minute," he said, eyebrows raised. "If you guys were so perfect for each other, then why did you leave us?"

"La-loyd, I didn't leave you," Garmadon said. "Sometimes life is complicated." He gave Lloyd a long, sad look. "Our love bloomed," he went on. "We were unstoppable. I thought we were going to conquer the world together. It was the happiest time of my life." He sighed happily, remembering the good times. "Then we came upon Ninjago City . . ."

The ninja hung on Garmadon's every word. This was a story they had never heard before.

"I thought Ninjago City was perfect," Garmadon said. "I told Koko I wanted to build our son's future on the ashes of that fine city." He looked at Lloyd. "After all, you had just been born . . . son."

Lloyd nodded.

"But it was at that moment," Garmadon continued, "that your mother realized the life of a conquering warlord was not the life she wanted . . . for *you*." Garmadon tried to keep his face still as he recalled the moment he lost his family forever. "And before I knew it, she was gone. And you, La-loyd, were gone, too."

The ninja all drew in a breath.

Lloyd couldn't believe what he was hearing. "Wow," he said, shaking his head. "Talk about spinning my perspective. Mom sacrificed everything for me. And I always thought you left us."

The other ninja stepped away from Lloyd and Garmadon, realizing they should give them a few minutes to talk privately. Besides, they had an Ultimate *Ultimate* Weapon to find.

"La-loyd," Garmadon said seriously once they were alone. "I know I haven't always been the best

father to you, but your mom was the best. She expected the best of me. And she only ever wanted the best for you. I guess I'm just now realizing how much I've always regretted letting you and your mother walk out of my life. I never should have let you go. But look at what an amazing ninja you've become. It's really hard to destroy you . . ." He ruffled Lloyd's hair. ". . . you little rascal."

"Garmadon," Lloyd said, taken aback. "Remember when I said 'I wish you weren't my father'? Well, I —"

"Lloyd!" Nya's excited shout came from down the hall, cutting them off. "I think we found the Ultimate *Ultimate* Weapon!"

"Jackpot!" Garmadon cheered. The moment between father and son was lost.

Lloyd and Garmadon followed the other ninja's excited voices. Down the hall, they came to a bedroom. The room — which was obviously the bedroom Master Wu and Garmadon had shared as children — had walls that were covered in sports pennants. Pressed against the far wall of the room was a set of bunk beds.

"It's over there," Nya said, pointing to the bed.

Garmadon strode confidently over to the bottom bunk and flipped over the mattress. Underneath, there was a long, rectangular box.

"Whoa!" Lloyd gasped. Clearly, this was where Master Wu had been hiding the Ultimate *Ultimate* weapon for many years. Under his bed!

Garmadon lifted the box that contained the Ultimate *Ultimate* Weapon. Then he pulled Lloyd to the side. "Listen," he said softly. "Let's use this thing against the Six-Toed Beast from regions beyond. Me and you —"

"You and me?" Lloyd said, his eyes bright.

"Side by side —" Garmadon continued.

"That sounds great!" Lloyd said.

"You're in?" Garmadon asked.

Lloyd grinned. "Super in."

"This will be our first battle together," said Garmadon.

"As father and son!" Lloyd said.

"As father and General Number One!" said Garmadon at the exact same moment.

"What?" Lloyd snapped, his eyes blazing. "I don't want to be your General Number One!"

Garmadon was trying to pin a gold star to Lloyd's shirt. But Lloyd shoved the star away.

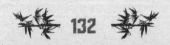

"No!" Lloyd said, hurt. "I don't *want* to be your General Number One. All I want is for you to be *my dad*!"

"Wait a minute," Garmadon said, confused. "You don't want to be my General Number One?"

"No," Lloyd said, shaking his head. "You don't get it. I thought we were gonna be father and son."

"Oh, no," Garmadon said. "I need a General Number One."

"I thought you had changed," Lloyd said, his shoulders slumping. "But you're obviously still the same warlord I always thought you were."

"That's right," Garmadon said lightly. "A warlord's gotta warlord. So . . . I guess I'll be taking my Ultimate *Ultimate* Weapon and conquering Ninjago all by myself." Garmadon hoisted the box over his shoulder.

"You're not going anywhere," Lloyd said, reaching for the Ultimate *Ultimate* Weapon.

"Oh, yeah?" Garmadon hissed. "Who's going to stop me? *You*, La-loyd?"

Cole, Jay, Kai, Nya, and Zane had been watching Lloyd and Garmadon as their conversation turned into an argument. Nya was the first to step forward, but the other ninja were right behind her.

133

"Lloyd ... and the rest of the Secret Ninja Force!" Nya growled.

"Stand down," Lloyd told his teammates. "He's my dad. This is my fight."

"Ha!" Garmadon cackled. "Do your worst, kid."

Lloyd and Garmadon each grabbed one end of the box and began tugging it back and forth. Garmadon kicked Lloyd in the stomach, sending him sprawling to the ground. But Lloyd jumped up quickly and charged at Garmadon again.

"You're making a mistake, La-loyd," Garmadon said between punches. "If we join forces, we would be unstoppable. Ninjago City would be ours. Just like I always wanted."

Lloyd and Garmadon threw punch after punch at each other. Garmadon dodged and weaved, trying to avoid Lloyd's rapid-fire blows. If he weren't so annoyed, he would probably have been proud of what a solid fighter his son had become.

"You'll never conquer Ninjago," Lloyd yelled. "Because I'll always be there to stop you!"

Garmadon chuckled. "You may have inherited your mom's sick moves, La-loyd, but you didn't inherit *this*." He lunged forward, throwing a punch that knocked out Lloyd and the rest of the ninja in

one swipe. With a laugh, he swept the Ultimate *Ultimate* Weapon box into his arms.

As he headed out the door, he called over his shoulder, "I'm really disappointed in you, La-loyd. You don't think I've changed? Before, I would have just locked you in here."

Garmadon grabbed the door handle and began to swing it closed. "Now I'm locking you in here, but feeling slightly guilty about it."

With that, he slammed the door shut. Garmadon hurried out of the temple and hopped into the helicopter. "So long, suckers!" he bellowed as he flew away.

Garmadon was heading straight toward Ninjago City — with the Ultimate *Ultimate* Weapon in tow!

19

As soon as Garmadon was gone, the temple began to shake and shudder. "What's that?" Nya asked.

"This doesn't look good," Jay said, covering his head.

Debris fell all around them, and a second later, the room began to cave in. It was an avalanche!

"Run!" Lloyd screamed.

The six ninja ran out of the temple, narrowly escaping before the walls and ceiling caved in completely.

But as soon as they reached the front door, they screeched to a stop. The stairs to the temple were gone, and the door opened onto nothingness. The ninja were teetering at the top of a cliff.

The whole mountain was gone. They were stranded on the top of a rocky precipice.

Before they could come up with a plan, a

familiar voice called out from somewhere nearby. "Jump, Lloyd!"

The ninja all looked around in disbelief — but they didn't see anyone.

"Master Wu?!" Lloyd asked.

"Trust me," Master Wu yelled to him. "Just jump!"

With no other options, Lloyd and the ninja listened to their master's voice. One by one, they jumped into nothingness.

Just as they began to fall, Lloyd's Mech Dragon swooped out of nowhere. All six ninja landed safely on its back.

"Ooh," Master Wu said, smiling at his team from the back of the dragon. "Nice jump."

"Master Wu!" the ninja cheered.

"You're alive!" Lloyd said happily.

"Yes, students," Master Wu said calmly. "This was my plan all along. Even the falling into the river part."

"You kids okay back there?" asked another familiar voice.

Only then did Lloyd wonder who was actually *steering* his mech.

"Mom?!" he said incredulously. Sure enough, Koko was working the control board. "But how'd you know —"

Nya leaned forward. "Oh my gosh, Lady Iron Dragon, can I just say I'm your number one fan?" she gushed.

"I'm a big fan of yours, too," Koko said, smiling.

"Your mom is *so* cool," Nya told Lloyd.

"Yeah," Lloyd agreed, giving his mom a hug. "You are pretty cool, Mom."

"Hate to break up this hug, but we need to bounce," Kai announced.

"You're right," Lloyd said. "And I've got a plan to get that Six-Toed Beast out of our city. Time to go into *stealth mode*!" he told the others.

"*NINJA-GO!*" the ninja cheered.

Koko let out a ninja battle cry. She steered the Dragon Mech sharply toward the ground. "Hold on to your ninja pants, 'cause we're coming in hot!"

When Garmadon returned to Ninjago City, he was pleased to see that the creature summoned forth by the Ultimate Weapon had continued to terrorize citizens and destroy buildings in his absence. The Six-Toed Beast stomped through the city, scattering people and stirring up embers and smoke and debris.

"Whoa," Garmadon said, hovering over the city in his copter. He patted the box that contained the Ultimate *Ultimate* Weapon. "Lucky for me, I've got you," he said sweetly.

He steered the helicopter to the roof of Ninjago Tower, and then dismounted with the box in tow. "One hot, steaming Ultimate *Ultimate* Weapon, made to order," he said, cackling.

Smoke hung over the city, low and thick. The ninja, Master Wu, and Koko landed in Ninjago City just as Garmadon set his helicopter down on the top of Ninjago Tower.

"Garmadon is on top of Ninjago Tower and he is waving the Ultimate *Ultimate* Weapon box around like a maniac," Zane said, scanning the city.

"Great," Lloyd said. "That will distract the beast and give us the chance to sneak up on him. Ready, guys?"

"Stealth mode," the other ninja whispered. "*NINJA-GO!*"

The ninja leaped from bush to bench, criss-crossing the city. To shield themselves from the prying eyes of the public, they smeared mud on their faces and covered themselves in sticks and vines.

"What are you doing?" Master Wu asked.

"We're camouflaging ourselves," Nya explained. "Because —"

"It's so NINJA!" the others whooped.

Master Wu nodded. "You've learned your lessons well. There is everything ninja about you ninja."

Koko beamed at the Secret Ninja Force. "Aw,

it's their very first stealth mission," she cooed. "I gotta take a photo. Everyone say 'NINJA'!"

The ninja all struck fierce poses as Koko held up her camera. They grinned and called out, "Ninja!"

Then the ninja snapped back into action. They could hear Garmadon calling out to the beast from the top of the tower.

"Here I am, beasty beast!" the evil warlord beckoned. "Come to Garma-daddy!"

"Look," Lloyd said, pointing to the top of the tower. "Garmadon's got the beast distracted. Now's our time to strike. Okay, guys, let's get rid of that monster . . . in the most humane way possible!"

"*NINJA-GO!*" the other ninja cried.

"Hey, look!" a citizen yelled as the ninja raced toward the tower. "It's the ninja!"

Everyone nearby cheered — until they spotted Lloyd, the Green Ninja, who was responsible for unleashing the beast.

"Wait a minute," someone said, frowning. "The Green Ninja is with them."

A rude chorus of boos echoed through the city.

143

"Don't listen to them, Lloyd," Master Wu said kindly. "Focus on your inner balance."

Lloyd smiled. He knew it was time to show everyone they were wrong about him!

"Thanks, Master Wu," he said. "I got this."

A top Ninjago Tower, Garmadon was ready to unleash the Ultimate *Ultimate* Weapon. He waved the box around in the air, waiting for the beast to approach.

"Ha!" Garmadon said, chuckling as the beast came face-to-face with the great warlord. He began to lift the box's lid, keeping his eyes trained on the creature. "You think you scare me? I have you right where I want —"

Before Garmadon could open the box and deploy the mighty weapon, the creature snatched Garmadon up into its mouth.

"Gah!" Garmadon shrieked. "This isn't what I was expecting!"

Meanwhile, down on the ground, the ninja put their plan into action. They assembled into pyramid formation and began to spin.

Suddenly, a mighty wind kicked up around them, and the air began to vibrate and shimmer. The ninja pyramid rose up, shooting shafts of light in all directions.

As the citizens of Ninjago City watched in awe, bricks began to float up into the air. As the ninja spun, the bricks clicked into place. In just a few moments, they'd assembled a huge, powerful mech that was even larger than the Six-Toed Beast.

"Behold!" Lloyd cried. He steered the giant mech toward the massive creature, not realizing his father was tucked inside the beast's mouth. "Get out of Ninjago City!" Lloyd screamed.

The beast turned. When it saw the ninja's creation, the enormous creature began to panic. It started thrashing around, terrified, tearing down the few buildings that remained standing in Ninjago City.

"You're making it worse than it was before!" a terrified citizen cried out.

"I knew you would mess it up, Green Ninja," hollered someone else.

"Boo!" All around the city, people shouted insults at Lloyd.

The Six-Toed Beast flailed and rampaged through the city, crushing everything in its path in an effort to get away from the ninja's mech.

"Guys," Lloyd said desperately. His plan was a disaster — this wasn't how he'd thought this would go! "It's not working. The beast is too scared to find her way out of the city. She's destroying everything!"

The ninja worked quickly to break down the mech they'd built, but it was too late to reverse the damage they had done. The beast was now totally out of control, and there was no stopping her.

"Ninjago's lost," Nya said hopelessly. "It's over, guys. We gotta get out of here."

Just then, they heard Garmadon's terrified screams coming from inside the beast's mouth.

"Ugh!" Garmadon yelped. "Get me out of here! Somebody help me!"

"Dad?" Lloyd said, searching for the source of his father's voice.

When he realized Garmadon was inside the beast's mouth, Lloyd started toward them.

"Lloyd, let him go," Kai urged. "He's finally out of your life."

"Isn't that what you always wanted?" Nya asked.

"I . . ." Lloyd said, pausing. "I don't know anymore."

Lloyd gazed up at the huge beast. Suddenly, he had an idea. "Wait a minute. I just have to spin my perspective . . . I know what to do!" He turned to his friends. "Guys, get everybody out of here. Everyone, evacuate Ninjago City!"

The ninja began to help people clear out of the city. Meanwhile, Lloyd took a step toward the beast. Then another, and another.

When Zane realized what Lloyd was planning, he put his arm out to stop him. "Lloyd — what are you doing? You can't go near that thing. Wait."

"Zane," Nya called out. "Come on!" She and Jay pulled Zane to safety, but they left Lloyd behind. They knew there was no stopping him.

"Here, beast," Lloyd said timidly, stealthily making his way toward the creature. "That's a good beast. Calm down. It's all right. Stay right there, everything will be okay." He reached out a hand and touched the beast's foot, stroking it gently.

The creature began to calm down. "Good. Now, I know you're just scared. And deep down inside, you're good. I promise everything is going to be okay. Nice and easy . . ."

The creature was finally calm enough that Lloyd was able to slip onto its back. He sat astride the creature, and then leaned forward to say, "Hey, Dad?"

"Yes, La-loyd," Garmadon's muffled voice replied from inside the creature's mouth.

"Look, um," Lloyd began. "I'm sorry. When I said that I wish you weren't my father, I didn't really mean it. I just wish we didn't fight all the time."

Garmadon said nothing for a moment. Inside the beast's mouth, the evil warlord felt his eyes growing wet. He couldn't figure out what on earth was wrong with him. "Me, too," he said, trying to hold back the tears that were threatening to spill over. "Son."

Suddenly, Garmadon's tears began to flow. And — just like he'd promised — they were made of fire!

The fiery tears spilled down his face, and then dripped onto the beast's tongue.

The creature hissed at the searing pain. She opened her mouth and spit Garmadon out.

"Dad!" Lloyd said, grinning as his father spilled to the ground. "Thanks, beast."

"La-loyd," Garmadon ordered as soon as he was back on his feet. "Get off that beast right now!"

But Lloyd had no intention of taking orders from his father. This was *his* battle now!

"Let's turn you around," Lloyd told the beast gently. "We'll just get you back home, all right?"

Koko had stayed behind in Ninjago City. She was determined to rescue her son. She raced toward Lloyd and Garmadon. "Lloyd!" she called out.

"It's okay," Lloyd said, waving. "I got this, Mom."

"Lloyd!" Koko screamed. "No!"

"It's okay," Lloyd said again. He nodded. "I have to do this."

He gently steered the Six-Toed Beast toward a giant portal that had opened up over the city. Just as Lloyd and the beast were about to disappear through the hole in the sky, Lloyd let go.

A moment later, the beast slipped through the portal. It was gone.

Lloyd plummeted back toward Ninjago City — falling down, down, down to the earth below.

"We gotta do something!" Nya screamed. She and the other ninja were on the outskirts of the city, watching helplessly as their teammate tumbled through the air.

Cole, Jay, Kai, Nya, and Zane raced toward Lloyd, but they were too far away. They would never get there in time.

Suddenly, Garmadon and Koko jumped off the edge of Ninjago Tower. With a mighty howl, they both reached out their arms and grabbed for their son.

"Gotcha!" Garmadon said as he and Koko caught Lloyd in their arms.

Together, Lloyd, Koko, and Garmadon fell the rest of the way to the ground.

"I'm never going to let you go again," Garmadon said, squeezing Lloyd against his chest.

On Lloyd's other side, Koko hugged her son tightly, shielding him from impact. The three of them plinked to the ground, bouncing a few times before coming to rest in the center of the destroyed city.

Lloyd took a mental inventory of his body, deciding that nothing was broken. His parents both seemed okay, too.

"Um, Dad," Lloyd said softly.

"Yes?" Lord Garmadon asked, still clutching his son in his arms.

"You can let go now," Lloyd told him.

"Thanks, son," Garmadon murmured, still holding tight. "I know."

"Lloyd, thank goodness you're okay," Koko said, her voice filled with raw emotion. She smiled at him, gently patting his hair into place. "Next time you save the city, can you at least wear a helmet?"

"You got it, Mom," Lloyd said, grinning. He got to his feet. "And Mom? Thanks for always being there for me."

Garmadon sighed as he gazed at Koko fondly. "Didn't I tell you your mother is the best, La-loyd?"

Suddenly, swarms of Ninjago City citizens surrounded the happy family. They rushed forward, lifting Lloyd over their heads. "We love you, Lloyd! You saved our city!" they chanted.

"Way to go, Lloyd," the other ninja said, giving their teammate high fives.

"I guess your dad's not a total monster," Zane said.

Another swarm of Ninjago City residents lifted Koko and Garmadon high above their heads. As the group of heroes were paraded around the city, the people of Ninjago City sang out: "*Everybody have a ninja day!*"

Garmadon grinned. "I guess conquering isn't the only way to feel good." He put all four of his hands in the air and pumped his fists. Then he glanced over at Lloyd. "Well, son. I guess I'll see you soon. Same time, same place?"

Lloyd nodded, his smile bigger than ever. He had done it — he'd saved Ninjago *and* he'd fixed his relationship with his father. He was definitely having a ninja day!

"Okay, Dad," Lloyd said with a wink. "But this time . . . I'm coming to your island."

BUILD YOUR
THE LEGO®
NINJAGO®
MOVIE™
LIBRARY!